Twisted Pathways of Murder & Death
A short story collection by
Rebecca Besser

"A short story is like a slice of pie. You know the slice is part of something bigger, but it's portioned out to make it easier to digest."

~ Rebecca Besser

Table of Contents

Bonus Stories

DEADLY MISTAKES

People kept going in and coming out of the red brick building that housed the lawyer's offices. People who didn't know they were getting screwed, trusting a stranger with their lives. It was such a stupid choice since the outcome was hanging in the balance of an unjust system. What a joke the entire law system was. They didn't help anyone. They let killers go free. Lawyers, judges, courts, laws – it was all a load of crap!

Hoping that no one would notice a middle-aged man entering through the glass doors with the embossed letters saying, 'Mathis Attorney at Law,' Charles Gross strode into the waiting area.

His business man's appearance was fooling them. Smiling politely and opening the door for a woman that was leaving, he looked around. No one even gave him a second glance. His average height, medium build, and short greying-brown hair made him invisible. Either that, or people were all self-absorbed and didn't care about anyone else. The woman didn't even say thank you to him for holding the door. All the people in the building seemed to be full of themselves.

Standing by the door for a moment, he let his eyes adjust to the dimmer interior of the bustling law office. Two people were sitting in the waiting area.

Two people's lives dangling in the balance of justice; today he planned to help the balance even out.

Charles took a seat on a swank couch, waiting until everyone left except for the receptionists. . .legal assistants, whatever they called themselves.

Busy, behind a massive half-moon shaped polished wood desk, they passed papers to each other and shared jokes. They didn't even notice he was there.

Their absorption in each other and their joking annoyed him intensely.

He couldn't help the inner rant tearing through his brain: *Wasn't he a person? Didn't they realize that he had feelings too? Who the heck did they think they were?* The giggling self-absorbed twits didn't care about anyone but themselves, it seemed to him. In his mind they couldn't be more obvious about how little he mattered to them.

Standing, Charles walked calmly over to the desk, waiting patiently to be noticed by the three young women. He studied them while he stood there.

One was a young petite blonde, with ringlet curls that reflected the light every time she moved her head. She had deep blue eyes that twinkled like she was continually laughing at you. The woman to her right had dark red hair that danced like fire. She was tall and had jade-green eyes that looked misty and secretive. To her right sat a short, slightly plumb girl with long dark brown hair that was pulled up in a ponytail. Her eyes were as dark as coal, and looked like they hid many secrets.

Which one was it? he wondered, as he watched them. *Which one made the mistake?*

He stood there, observing them for a minute or more. Finally, the petite blonde glanced up and saw him standing there.

"Oh, hi," she chirped happily. "Can I help you? Do you have an appointment?"

"No. I don't have an appointment," Charles said, smiling broadly. "I think you can help me."

He let his eyes flick from her to the other two women, typing on their keyboards, and then returned his attention to her. Reaching inside his dark gray suit jacket, as if to retrieve a letter or a business card, he held her gaze. Instead of paper Charles pulled out a cool length of steel. In his hand he held a .45 caliber revolver. Cocking the hammer, he slid his finger onto the trigger, leveling the barrel at the blonde's head.

The smile vanished from her pixie face. Fear shone from her deep blue eyes and her bottom lip quivered.

Aw, the satisfaction of revenge, he thought, forcing himself to keep a straight face.

"Actually, I think you can all help me," he announced, raising his voice so all three receptionist could hear him. "First, I want you all to unplug the phone lines from the back of your phones. Slowly now, no one wants to get hurt."

They did as they were told. He couldn't help but laugh at their ignorance and fear. *Little robots,* he thought, *they have turned from nitwit giggling women into robots in an instant.*

"Is there anyone in the offices?" he asked the redhead.

"N. . .no," she stuttered. "They're out to lunch."

"Well, that's fine with me," he said with a mocking grin. "I came to see you ladies."

Charles' heart danced happily in his chest as they gripped each other's hands and whimpered. He wanted them to suffer, to feel how terrifying it was for a woman to be at the mercy of a deranged man. . .to have to do whatever they were told. He wanted them to fear for their very lives.

"Now, I want you all to clear your computer screens. We're gonna play a little game."

They glanced at each other, their eyes brimming with fear.

Was that how she'd looked in the end? he wondered fleetingly, swallowing hard against a lump in his throat. *My beautiful wife, my August.*

He almost lost his nerve to go on, as their hands shook while they obeyed his orders. He couldn't hear anything but his own heart beating; it seemed to be pounding ten times faster than normal. There was a strange roaring in his ears, and the room began to spin around him. Closing his eyes, he fought for control. *My wife wasn't given any mercy and neither will they*, he resolved.

Looking at them through his unshed tears he knew he had to do this. . .for her. She needed to be vindicated. She deserved so much more. She deserved to be here with him, still living their happy life. Not abused, and dead, left in some dirty alley.

"Now, I want you to open whatever program you use to type up letters. Here are the rules of the game."

Charles' voice was husky with the struggle to contain his emotions. His pain and anger warred. He wanted to end this right now, to not even give them a sliver of a chance. But that would have been sinking to *his* level. That evil man. . .he would never be anything like *him*. Relaxing his grip on the gun, and taking a deep breath, he calmed his violent urges.

Pausing, he took an envelope out of his jacket, handing it to the blonde.

"What's your name, blondie?" he asked with overly polite sarcasm that dripped with his blatant disgust of her.

"Wendy," she whimpered, taking the envelope with a trembling hand.

"Wendy, there are three copies of a letter in that envelope," he continued with the same mock politeness. "Please hand one to each of the other ladies and keep one for yourself."

Wendy did as she was told – fear kept her obedient.

Amazing how that works, he thought to himself smugly.

"It's time to tell you more about the fun game we're going to play," Charles announced, swinging the gun at each woman, just to show he meant business. "You will each type the letter into your computer. If you make any mistakes, you will die. It's as simple as that. If you can type the whole letter without typos, you live."

He laughed at the confused looks on their faces; even to his own ears it sounded harsh, and mirthless.

"Do you have any questions before we start?" he asked. "I would hate for you to die because you didn't understand the game."

Charles' voice dripped with sarcasm and he really just wanted to end it all. He wanted to end them, and end his own pain. He just wanted to be with his precious August again, to be happy. He wanted to see her smile. He wanted to feel her beside him in bed when the darkness fell on the world. He wanted to know that she would be there when he awoke in the morning. God help him, but he missed her more than he ever thought was possible.

The redhead raised her hand slightly.

He gestured to her with the gun, his hand shaking slightly. He hoped they didn't notice.

"You! What's your name?" he asked.

"Summer," she said softly.

"What's your question, Summer?" He practically screamed at her, and was rewarded with a cringe.

"Why. . .why are you doing this to us?" she asked.

"Good question. Good question, Summer," he said, as he laughed mockingly. "Let me explain. Three months ago this firm was involved in the prosecution of a man named, Maxwell Allen. You remember. . .the one who killed that family while they slept. Killed them all in cold blood. Well, to make a long story short, he was set free because of some typo, on some document. An important document apparently! The typo originated from this office, and one of you typed it! Which one of you, and which document, I don't know! So, I thought up this game to give you each a chance. Any more questions?"

Glancing at each other, the third woman raised her hand.

"Yes. You! Who might you be?"

He didn't even recognize the voice that was speaking. It was so harsh and hateful that it scared even him. *How could I become someone that would do something like this?* he wondered inside. He decided it didn't matter now; it was too late to turn back.

"Rachel," she said, her voice quivering.

"What's your question, Rachel?"

Charles sneered at her, pointing the gun at her head, leaning against the desk to intimidate her. He was surprised she had the nerve to continue.

"But. . .but why are you doing this?" Rachel asked. "Were the people who were killed related to you?"

He thought he saw a flicker in her eyes, something akin to sadness or sympathy. *No,* he decided, *I must be imagining it. These women didn't care about people. They let people get hurt, because they're careless!*

"Let's see," he said, tapping the barrel of the gun against his lips in a thoughtful gesture. "Yes, and no. No, I wasn't related to the family that was murdered in their sleep."

"I was," he shouted, shaking the gun at them, "married to the woman Maxwell Allen raped and killed last month. Fortunately for him, he was shot when he pulled a gun on an officer that was trying to arrest him! But my wife is still dead, because one of you stupid, self-centered, excuses for women, can't type! He was on the streets and attacked my wife, because of your mistake with the family murder case!"

The room was completely silent. All three of the women's eyes were pools of terror. They knew he was going to do what he said. Any small shred of hope they might have been holding onto was now gone.

"Okay, it's time to start," he announced in a falsely calm voice. "You will all start at the same time, so it's all fair. When the second hand reaches the twelve, you will begin." He motioned to the clock with the barrel of the gun.

All eyes turned to the huge clock that hung on the wall, to the left of the desk. Its massive hands ticked by the seconds, reaching the eleven.

Tick, five. *Tick*, four. *Tick*, three. *Tick*, two. *Tick*, one.

"Begin!" Charles yelled.

The only sound that could be heard was the *click*ing of keys as the women's fingers typed rapidly. Their eyes were trained on the papers in front of each of them, occasionally looking up at their screens.

He moved behind the desk, glancing from screen to screen, watching for mistakes.

BANG!

The two girls jumped as Wendy's head fell forward onto the desk. She was dead. Blood ran from the hole in her temple, onto its polished wood surface. Brain matter was splattered all over the desk and her computer. Her deep blue eyes no longer sparkled, but stared sightlessly at the other two women.

"One down," he said.

Charles' voice no longer carried even a shred of emotion. He was frozen inside. He thought it would feel better than this. *Maybe, after this is over,* he hoped, *I'll feel some satisfaction.*

"Keep typing," he commanded.

They turned back to the letter and their computers with tears streaming down their faces. Fingers flew over keyboards, and the *click*ing of keys echoed in the quiet room.

BANG!

Rachel screamed. She glanced up as Summer's body slid to the floor with a *thud*. Blood ran freely from the hole in her head out onto the carpet.

"It's just you now, Rachel," Charles stated calmly. "Keep typing."

Rachel was shaking as she turned her attention back to her task. Every few key strokes a sob escaped her throat.

"If you make it through with no mistakes, you'll live."

Time passed slowly as Rachel sobbed and typed.

He stood over her, watching the screen like a hawk watches a mouse before it strikes.

She finished the letter and lowered her shaking hands into her lap.

BANG!

Thump. The body hit the floor. Rachel opened my eyes to see the man's body lying beside Summer's.

She felt instantly sick, throwing up in the closest trash can.

After reattaching the phone line with numb fingers, she dialed 9-1-1.

"9-1-1 emergency, how can we assist you?"

The sound of the dispatcher's voice made her grip the phone with relief. Help was coming now, but it was a little too late.

"I need police."

"What is the nature of you emergency, ma'am?"

Taking deep breaths, Rachel found her voice to reply.

"A man… A man came into the office, and killed them. Summer and Wendy – they're dead," she stammered into the phone.

"I need you to calm down and speak clearly into the mouth piece. What is your name, and where are you? I'm showing the Mathis Law Office. Is that your location?"

"Yes, that's where I am," she said, speaking slowly. The room was spinning and she felt light headed.

"Ma'am? MA'AM!"

The dispatcher's urgent voice brought her back to the present.

"Yes. . ." Rachel replied weakly.

"What's your name? We have officers on the way. Talk to me while you wait. I need to know if there is anyone there, anyone threatening you. You need to try to calm down and tell me what is going on."

"My, my name is Rachel. I, I work as a receptionist at the Mathis Law Office." She paused, swallowed hard, and closed her eyes. She couldn't think straight, looking at all the pain and death around her. "A man came into the office. He had a gun. He made us, made us play a game. He made us type a letter. If we made any mistakes, he said he would kill us."

"Okay," the dispatcher sounded sympathetic, but urgent now. "Is the man with the gun where you can see him? Is he still threatening you?"

"No. No, he's dead. He shot. . ." her voice cracked, and tears started running down her face again. "He shot the two girls that work with me, and then he shot himself. I'm the only one here. The only one here, alive."

Slowly the room got dark, and the dispatcher's voice became more and more distant. Rachel's lips felt stiff and numb, and her hands started to shake.

~ * ~

The next thing Rachel knew she was laying on something soft, and someone was slapping her face gently, calling her name.

"Rachel, you need to wake up. Come on, wake up, Rachel!"

She opened her eyes a sliver, and suddenly a bright light appeared. A strange man was shining the light into her eyes, holding her forehead. He was kneeling beside the couch she was laying on, looking at her with concern.

"You passed out, Rachel," he said. "You hit your head on the edge of the desk. You might have a concussion. We need to take you to the hospital to check you out."

He had a really kind voice, and he seemed genuinely concerned.

"No, I don't want to go to the hospital," she mumbled in a slurred, weak voice. "Want to go home."

"I really advise against that, Ma'am," the nice paramedic said gently, but sternly. "You need to be looked after. You need to be checked out, to make sure there's no lasting or more serious injury to your skull."

"No," she insisted with a little more strength. "No. Going home."

She moved to sit up, but fell back against the couch with a moan.

"You really should seek professional attention," the persistent man said, watching her intently. "But, I can't force you. If you don't wish to go to the hospital, you'll have to sign a waiver, saying that you were advised, and refused to seek professional attention."

"Fine," she sighed, willing to do anything, just to make everything go away, even if it was only for a second.

She heard a rustling of papers and a few low murmurs.

She forced herself to sit up, despite the room's need to spin in a circle.

Taking the offered paper, Rachel signed where she was told. Then came the questions from the police. She gave her statement and was soon on her way home.

All the questions and answers became a blur in her mind, as she concentrated on driving the short distance home. An officer was following her to make sure she made it home safe. She wasn't supposed to be driving, but they had finally agreed to allow her the trip, and insisted on the tail.

~ * ~

When Rachel opened the door to her quiet apartment, her eyes went to a picture hanging on the wall. The picture was of her sister and her sister's family – the family that had been murdered by Maxwell Allen.

She fell to my knees and wept.

"Oh, sis, why do people think that is okay to hurt others because they're hurting? I was hoping the violence would end when that man was shot by the police. But he seems to be able to reach from the grave to tear even more of my life apart."

Sob after sob wracked her body, until she fell asleep on the floor, worn out from all the pain. It was unbelievable how one person could cause so much suffering in people's lives.

TURN OF EVENTS

The nurse left work at five o'clock. She rushed to make it to the store, and then home in time to make supper. She wanted to make it home before her husband got hungry – he was mean when he was hungry. Of course there was no reason he couldn't go to the store and get what they needed and make supper. Other than he'd become a lazy drunk and he would have bought more booze. If he bought more alcohol, he would more than likely end up passing out, or worse, staying awake just to smack her around again.

Their life hadn't always been this way; it was only after the factory closed, moving to China, that he'd become like this. He'd lost all hope when he couldn't find work and that in turn had eaten the good away inside him. The man that she'd married was nothing more than a figment of her imagination now.

She drove home as fast as traffic allowed, running one red light and almost causing an accident in the process. The near-miss added strain to her already fraying nerves. By the time she pulled into her assigned parking space in the apartment parking lot, her hands were shaking and she was almost panicked.

She quickly grabbed the groceries from the trunk of her car and headed up the stairs to their small apartment. Struggling with the bags, she unlocked the door, almost dropping the bags and her keys in her awkward haste.

She made her way to the kitchen with no further incident and set her load down on the table.

The sound of the TV droned at a sedate volume from the living room. She could faintly make out the news broadcast as they talked about the downward spiral of the economy and the unemployment rate rising.

As quietly as possible, she walked to the archway leading from the hallway to the living room. She saw her husband asleep on the couch when she peeked around the corner. She stepped gingerly into the room, picked the remote control up off the coffee table, and turned off the TV. She set the remote back down gently and turned to head back to the kitchen. When she again reached the archway, she breathed a sigh of relief. He hadn't woken up or even moved while she was in there. His deep slumber gave her a measure of peace, knowing that he hadn't been sitting there waiting for her, stewing up an underserved anger and thinking up an unjust punishment for her.

She set to work making supper – each movement and process calming her down more and more until her nerves had calmed and she was no longer shaking.

She jumped as she heard a noise behind her. Turning she saw her husband standing in the doorway, watching her. She laughed at herself for being startled, and smiled at him.

"Did you get more beer?" he asked in a flat tone.

"No," she whispered, instantly on edge again.

He swore and advanced toward her. Grabbing her arm, he shook her roughly.

She stiffened and let all her facial muscles go lax to erase her features of any expression at all. She wouldn't meet his gaze, but stared down at nothing.

"Don't you ever use your brain?" he snapped, shaking her hard again.

She didn't answer.

He backhanded her; the strike sounded as loud as a gunshot in the small room.

Her head snapped back from the impact and she cried out in pain. No matter how she tried to keep quiet, the pain always made something slip out and she felt all the weaker for it.

He continued shaking her, moving her closer and closer to the stove. Her back slammed into the counter with a loud *bang*. She felt her knees buckle. Dangling from his grip like a rag doll, she tried to catch her breath.

"Please stop," she whimpered, looking into his cold eyes with her tear-filled ones; she tried to use all of her feelings and emotions to convince him not to hurt her more.

She heard the hiss of water hitting a hot electric burner as he moved a pan aside. He tugged her arm closer and closer to the glowing rings.

"No!" she screamed.

He grinned at her sadistically and yanked her arm harder.

Frantically, she groped for the counter with her other hand; her fingers fell on the knife she'd used to chop vegetables for their meal. Without thinking – in a blind panic – she arched up and thrust the knife into the side of his neck.

Blood sprayed through the air and landed on the half-prepared meal she'd been making for them. He staggered backwards, releasing her arm to clutch at his wound. He fell, knocking over a chair and landing flat on his back on the tiled floor. His life fluid continued to flow from his throat and pooled in an almost black puddle underneath him until he stopped breathing.

She slid to the floor with her back against the cabinets. Her scrubs were covered with her husband's blood. She couldn't believe what had just happened – what she'd done.

She stared at her husband's body. With a shudder she thought about how they had gotten to this point.

"I'm sorry," she whispered, covering her face with her hands. "I'm so, so, so sorry! Maybe...if the economy hadn't taken a turn for the worst and the factory hadn't moved – and you still had a job and self-worth – then we'd still be happily married, dreaming about kids and a future."

STALKERS BEWARE

Mitchell Peterson stood backstage with a knot of anticipation growing inside his chest as he listened to the crowd gather for the concert. It didn't matter how many times he and his band took the stage, it still excited him. Adrenaline would spike his system and he'd be a music making machine for hours on end. But the music wasn't the only thing that got him going; there were all the girls – groupies by the dozens who wanted a piece of him and everyone else on stage. Being wanted that badly took the high to another level.

After lifting his guitar and sliding on the shoulder strap, he peeked out at the people who were settling into their seats, waiting anxiously for their appearance. He scanned the audience looking for just the right one. He saw *her* sitting in the second row off to the left of the stage.

The woman he'd spotted had long, curly, darkish blonde hair that hung loose around her shoulders. She was wearing a white tank top with the band's name stretched taunt across her generous breasts and a pair of black jeans that fit her perfectly.

"You ready, man?" a gruff voice asked from behind him.

Mitch turned to see Dave, the drummer for the band. He smirked, "Ready as always."

The two men laughed. *Ready as always*, was their theme for music and women. Having traveled from gig to gig together for months, they'd become as close as brothers. Mitch sometimes felt closer to the people he traveled with than his own family. At least they understood the driving need to create, to keep moving, and to make something of himself and his name. They were all in this together and they understood him like no one else could, or would. Sometimes he thought people just didn't want to take the time to understand him, too busy with their own mundane matters.

The lights dimmed and the men looked at each other, grinning broadly, each making a fist and bumping their knuckles together before they charged out on stage as they were announced.

"I present to you, Wane of Existence!"

The screams and cheers of the crowd drowned out all other sound for almost an entire minute. Mitch closed his eyes and let his body absorb the sound and excitement of the crowd as he played the first chords of the opening song. He felt the music course through him, caressing his soul and setting it on fire. Feeling like he was free and weightless, he let it take him, carrying him beyond himself and what he could be to a place no one could touch him – he was in his zone.

Song after song, the concert went on. Mitch noted how the blonde woman watched him and screamed out his name and how much she loved him. She would be an easy mark. Most of the groupie-stalkers were, or else he wouldn't be able to feed his appetite. This particular one had been at every show in the area for the last six months. He'd even seen her at one of their out of state concerts. Every time, she tried to get backstage to see him, telling security she was his girlfriend.

Before he knew it, they were done and backstage. Mitch was almost surprised to find that he was covered with sweat, but it was something he'd come to expect; he'd be so fixated on his music, he wouldn't notice much of anything else. Downing bottle after bottle of water to sate his thirst, he started to think about the blonde and his hunger.

Mitch did his duty, signing autographs and talking to people who'd spent the extra money and bought back stage passes. But as he went through the motions, the blonde was on his mind. He hoped she'd try to get backstage again tonight, because he had plans for her.

She didn't disappoint. He grinned broadly when he spotted her and her friend talking to stage security, trying to convince the men to let them come backstage.

Excusing himself, he headed over and picked up some of the conversation.

"I'm sorry, ladies," one of the security men said. "Like I already said, we can't let you back there without a pass."

Mitch put his hand on the man's shoulder and said, "It's all right, would you ladies like an autograph?"

The women smiled at Mitch, nodded eagerly, and tried to press themselves up against him while he scrawled his name on what they wanted signed. He felt a hand slide into his back, left pants pocket and ignored it, allowing a small piece of paper to be withdrawn. After signing autographs, he allowed them to get their pictures taken with him, using their cell phones.

As they were walking away, he watched them closely, noting how the blonde withdrew something from her pocket and whispered to her friend, who looked shocked and amazed. His plan had worked like a charm. Now all he had to do was sit back and wait.

"What was that all about?" Dave asked. He'd noticed the exchange while he was talking to someone from the stage crew about when the equipment would need to be loaded and moved out.

"That crazy-blonde-stalker-chick was here again," Mitch said, as they walked together to the green room. "I thought maybe if I gave her an autograph she'd finally leave me alone."

Dave laughed. "Like that's ever going to happen! She'll follow your sexy ass around until the day she dies!"

Mitch grinned and twisted the top off another bottle of water. He didn't say anything about his plan to his friend – there were some things that didn't need to be shared. But Dave was right, she would follow him around until the day she died, that he was absolutely sure of.

"Speaking of stalkers," Craig – another member of the band – said. "What happened to that redhead who was after you for eight months, Mitch? I haven't seen her forever."

Mitch took a swallow of water and shrugged his shoulders. "Don't know. Maybe she found someone else to be obsessed about. Maybe she got knocked up by some guy and has to stay home now. How should I know?"

Craig laughed. "Yeah, maybe!"

Dave winked at Mitch and looked at Craig. "You're just jealous because you don't have any crazy bitches tryin' to crawl between your sheets and follow you to the bathroom!"

Craig scowled. "Shut up, fucker! I've got plenty of chicks wanting me, I just don't pay attention to them because I love Beth, and you know it."

Dave and Mitch laughed.

"Sure," Dave said. "That's what it is. . ."

Mitch smiled. "It's okay, Craig, not everyone can be as handsome as me. I'm blessed."

They all laughed, knowing Mitch got the most female attention because he was the most outgoing and charismatic man in the group, which they were okay with. After all, Dave was married and Craig was engaged. Troy, the only other member of the band, was shy and hid from the fans more often than not.

"Maybe you should start a groupie/stalker harem," Craig teased. "Then you could have all kinds of fun."

Mitch shook his head and finished his water. "While that sounds like fun and all, I don't want to die of some weird disease. Have you seen some of those women? They're scary!"

Dave smiled. "Very true. There have been some really scary ones following you around. How come all the pretty or decent ones disappear after a while, but the nasty ones are always around?"

"Probably because the decent ones figure out after a while that I'm just human like everyone else," Mitch said. "And the nasty ones can't get anyone to love them, so they have to dream about me."

Troy walked into the green room and heard the last comment. "Something like that," he said. "I think we're about ready to get out of here. . .How long will it take you guys to get your shit? I want to go home."

With that, they gathered their personal belongings and made sure everything was taken care of and loaded. They'd hired a crew to handle the equipment for this tour, which was nice. They keenly remembered the days when they'd had to set up and tear down their own stuff.

Finally on the bus heading toward home, Mitch had some time to think about his plan. If things went as smoothly as they normally did, he would be a very happy man in a night or two. Glancing at Troy, who was sitting on the built in couch reading a book, he wondered if he would be up for a double again. Troy was the only one he trusted to participate in his dark activities. After a few moments of thought, he shook his head, letting go of the idea. He wanted to enjoy it alone this time. It was always. . .*sweeter* somehow when he took care of things himself.

~ * ~

It was three o'clock in the morning when Mitch unlocked the door to his small house. He stumbled inside, kicked the door shut, and locked it. With a heavy, tired sigh, he hung his keys on the hook by the door and dropped his bag to the floor. Trudging into the kitchen, he extracted a beer from the fridge and opened it. Tossing the cap in the trash, he picked up the handset of his phone to check his voice mail. He would have preferred to go straight to bed, but after missing an important message once when a friend had been taken to the hospital, he now checked his messages right away.

He almost started laughing when he heard he had forty-five messages, betting most of them were left by the blonde. He was right. She'd called multiple times, leaving messages that ranged from pathetic to obscene. He'd been right on when he'd picked her.

After hanging up the phone, still laughing to himself, he downed the rest of his beer and went to take a shower. The hot water relaxed him to the point he almost fell asleep standing up. He turned off the water, stumbled out of the bathtub, quickly toweled dry, trudged into his bedroom, flopped onto the bed, and was instantly asleep.

~ * ~

When Mitch awoke it was last afternoon and his stomach was rumbling. Stretching, he got out of bed, pulled on underwear, baggy jeans, and a T-shirt while thinking about what he wanted to eat. He picked up the phone to order pizza and heard an insistent beep telling him he had more messages. *I must have been really tired*, he thought. He normally woke up when the phone rang. Absently, he punched in his pass code while looking into the depths of his empty refrigerator, trying to find something to snack on until he could get some decent food.

It was the blonde again. She'd left more obscene messages and they were giving him some wild ideas. With a sigh, he wrote down her number and deleted the messages. He dialed her number. After only two rings, she answered.

"Hello?" she practically purred in his ear.

"Hi, is Marcy there?" he asked in an offhand tone, knowing it was her without asking.

"This is her," she said, and giggled. "Who's this?"

"I think you know who this is," he teased, grinning. "You're a very bad girl, leaving all those naughty messages."

She giggled again. "Did you like them?"

"Yes, I did," he said. "Why do you think I'm calling?"

In less than two minutes, he set up a time and got her address to pick her up for a date that evening and then was off the phone.

"Too easy," he mumbled to himself.

Mitch found some microwave popcorn in a cabinet and decided it would have to do. He didn't want to spoil his appetite, looking forward to a filling meal later. He carried the bag with him, munching on the buttery snack while he mentally went over everything he would need later that night, checking to make sure it was in place. Everything was where it should have been and was ready. It had been months since he'd had a woman over, but he was meticulous with his preparations, so he didn't have to do much.

~ * ~

Hours later, Mitch rang the doorbell at the address he'd been given. Marcy answered the door looking lovely in a slutty sort of way. She wore entirely too much makeup, her skirt was a little too tight and short, and her shirt showed too much cleavage. It was all right with him, he wasn't taking her home to his parents, so he admired what she was so blatantly offering.

"Hi," she said, biting her bottom lip and looking him over.

"Hi, yourself," he said with an appreciative smile. "You ready?"

"Yup," she chirped, grabbed her purse, shut the door behind herself, and made sure she brushed up against him as she sauntered out to his car.

Mitch followed her slowly, watching and admiring the muscle tone of her legs and the firmness of her ass. He couldn't help but lick his lips in anticipation. Rushing forward, he opened the car door for her and was inwardly pleased to see her smile as she tucked her hair behind her ear while she climbed in. She was well on her way to trusting him, and he would need that trust later tonight if he was to get what he was after.

Walking briskly around the car, he slid in the driver's side and shut the door behind him. As he reached forward to turn the key in the ignition, she took a hold of his wrist and tugged it over until his hand was resting on her knee.

"What's your hurry?" she asked, leaning her head back against the headrest and arching her back like a content kitten, showing off her breasts.

He gently squeezed her knee, massaging the soft, warm skin of her leg with his fingertips. "I thought you might be hungry."

"Oh, I'm hungry," she purred, "for you." Sitting forward, she leaned over and kissed him on the lips, slowly and gently. Pulling back, she blinked her big grayish blue eyes at him. "Do you want to feed me?"

Mitch grinned. "If that's what you want."

She giggled before kissing him again.

He knew what she wanted. It was the same thing all the others had wanted, so he gave it to her. Thrusting his free hand into her hair, he kissed her back, hard. She whimpered, wrapped her arms around his neck, and tried to climb onto his lap, but he turned sideways to keep that from happening. She started to grope at him and claw at his clothes desperately and he had to force himself not to shove her away in disgust and tell her to get the hell out of his car. That wouldn't get him what *he* wanted, so he held back his natural reaction. Slowly, he pulled back and forced a smile.

"I'll give you that later," Mitch said, kissing her again. "Right now, we're going to go have dinner."

She whimpered and stuck her bottom lip out in a pout, but nodded. Sitting back in the passenger seat, she tried to adjust her ridiculously short shirt and look semi-decent.

Starting the car, Mitch looked in his mirrors to make sure nothing was coming and caught the look of steel in his own eyes. He was seething inside. He couldn't believe that most women didn't have any self-respect and thought the only way they could hold a man's interest was to throw their bodies at them. Shaking himself mentally, he refocused on what he was doing and the woman beside him, reminding himself of later and what was to come. Those thoughts easily brought a smile back to his face.

They made light, polite conversation as they traversed to the restaurant he'd chosen for dinner. It was out of the way and small, but they had good food. The meal seemed to fly by with Marcy constantly talking about all the stuff she thought musicians were interested in, just like all the others had. While it pleased him they were so interested in what he'd accomplished, he thought the absolute obsession and brainwashing – leaving no room for their own thoughts – was incredibly sad. Plus, they had no idea who he really was and only seemed interested in the surface stuff they *thought* he was. By the time the meal was over he was almost thoroughly depressed by his ultimate loneliness and disgusted by her hero worship attitude.

After they were both back in the car, he decided to move things along a little faster than he normally would have.

"I was going to take you to a movie, but I'm still a bit tired after the long tour," he said with a crooked grin. "Why don't we go back to my place and watch something there?"

Marcy's eyes brightened and she was completely pathetic in her eagerness to please. "Oh, that sounds great! Really!"

He drove them back to his house, knowing there would be no movie. He was right. As soon as they walked through the door, she practically threw herself at him. In no time flat she had her skirt off, showing off her red, see-through thong as she slipped off her shoes.

"How about I just put you to bed? Since you're so tired and all. . ." she said, wrapping her arms around his neck and standing on her tip toes to kiss him.

"Mmm," he murmured as he slid his hands down her back and cupped her bare ass, "that sounds like a great idea." She squealed as he squatted down slightly and gripped the backs of her legs behind her knees, lifting her and wrapping her legs around his waist. "But first, let's take a shower."

"Yes, babe," she breathed into his ear as she nibbled his earlobe, "anything you want."

In a frenzy of tearing off clothes and trying not to fall, they made their way down the hall and into the bathroom. Soon they were naked under the hot spray of the shower, enjoying each other vigorously.

"Tell me when you're coming," he growled against her slick, wet neck as he thrust into her.

She whimpered and begged him to fuck her, and he did. Her breath was coming in short, deep pants and he knew she was almost there. Reaching down to the handle bar above the soap dish, he yanked the circular tube hard and it popped out of its hold smoothly, just as she started crying out that she was having an orgasm. Lifting the tube above his head, he thrust his erection deep into her as hard as he could, becoming more excited by the moment, knowing what was about to happen and anticipating it with all of his being. He watched her face as her body shook with sexual pleasure, and at just the right moment, he stabbed the tube downward, sinking the blade attached to the handle deep into the side of her throat. Her eyes flew open as she cried out sharply for the last time. Ripping the knife back out, he buried his face in her neck, sucking and licking at the blood he'd spilt as he too came with intense pleasure.

After the rush of his climax eased slowly from his quivering body, Mitch became acutely aware of the spray of the shower falling over him and the limp, dead body of Marcy in his arms. With a smile, he laid her down on the floor of the shower and quickly washed himself off while she bled out. Soap suds and blood swirled together as they both raced down the drain and out of the tub. He'd learned long ago that making the kill in the shower was the best way. He liked it because he didn't end up with as much of a mess.

Turning off the shower, he carefully stepped out of the tub and toweled dry before opening the cabinet under the sink and extracting a large, folded sheet of clear plastic and a rolled up package of chefs' knives. He proceeded to unfold and lay the plastic on the floor – kneeling on it – and then he opened the roll of knives, looking over their pristine steel thoughtfully. Choosing a blade, he leaned into the tub and made a long, deep cut in Marcy's throat, pleased to see only a slight trickle of blood ooze from the new wound.

Having butchered women many times before, it took him only an hour and a half to get all the useful meat from Marcy's corpse. Leaving the meat in the tub, he lifted out her skeleton and lay in on the plastic sheet. Wiping the blood from his body on the damp towel he'd used to dry himself earlier, he looked down at what was left of his most recent dedicated stalker with a twisted grin on his face. She'd been incredibly easy and it wasn't as late at night as he'd anticipated when he'd done his planning. Meaning he also had time to dispose of her bones before bed. He hated leaving them lying around any longer than he had to. Living in the country and being surrounded by acres of forest, he had a lot of privacy, but he didn't want to take it for granted, just in case.

Stepping over the pile of death in his bathroom, he headed down the hall to his bedroom, where he donned a pair of sweat pants and an old, black T-shirt. Slipping on a pair of old, mud splattered sneakers, he headed back to the bathroom, now ready to take out the trash. The thought of the word 'trash' at this point always made him laugh. In his opinion he was taking out the trash of womankind. They were slutty, easy, and severely lacking in the self-respect and character that any human person should have. In some ways he viewed them as nothing more than animals – bitches in heat that he took care of and put out of their misery.

Dragging the tarp and shuffling backwards, even though it didn't weigh very much, Mitch made his way out the back door – pausing briefly to flip a switch that flooded his back yard with light – and continued across the porch, down the steps, and toward the wood pile. Once there, he yanked his axe out of the stump he used for splitting wood and got to work severing the bony limbs from the once life-filled woman. After he had them cut down into smaller, manageable pieces, he started up his gas powered wood chipper and struck the head of the axe back into the stump. Slowly, he fed the bones into the grinding part of the machine and watched them come out the other end in small, mulch-like chips. The noise was incredibly loud in the quiet evening, and the bright flood lights mounted on the back of the house would have made everything crystal clear had anyone been able to see back there. He'd put up a privacy fence shortly after moving in. At the time it was to keep the neighbors' dogs out of his yard, but when he'd started giving in to his dark urges, it had come in quite handy. He also knew the neighbors wouldn't think anything of the noise. He worked strange hours, and with band practice and concerts his schedule was erratic at the best of times. He'd often mulched fallen limbs late in the evening, even took the time to take care of fallen branches for his closest neighbors – almost half of a mile away – who were an elderly couple, both in their late eighties.

After all the bones were taken care of, he sent through a couple of four inch diameter limbs to clean out any meat or bits of bone that might have worked into the gears – they did their job well. Soon he was done mulching and he shut off the machine. The silence that surrounded him was almost eerie after the loud noise of the mulcher, but he delighted in it. He loved peace and quiet as much as he loved the noise and energy of being on stage.

He hummed one of the songs he was currently working on while he shoveled the bone/mulch mixture onto a larger heap of mulch sitting off to the side. Once they were added, he shoveled some of the old mulch over the new, knowing the bugs would eat whatever flesh was still there, and that the heat of the pile would dry the bone out faster.

Yawning and stretching, standing the shovel back against the fence from where he'd gotten it, he dragged the bloody plastic sheet over to the hose reel and unwound the hose. He lazily sprayed it off as if the red streaks were nothing more than paint. Once it was mostly clean, he went inside and retrieved a gallon of bleach. He dumped some on the tarp, sat the gallon jug on the steps so he wouldn't forget to take it back in when he went inside, and sprayed the plastic down again. When he was done, he hung the plastic over the rail of his porch and set a rock on each end to keep it from blowing away.

"Well, that didn't take long," he muttered to himself as he picked up the bleach and headed back inside. He took it with him and set it on the bathroom floor, knowing he would need it after he finished butchering and bagging the meat in the tub.

As he stepped into the kitchen, ready to open the fridge door and grab a beer, he almost jumped out of his skin when the phone rang, startling him. He snatched up the handset and pressed 'talk.'

"Hello. . ." he said, glancing at the clock on his microwave that said it was only a little after nine o'clock. "Oh, hi, Craig. No, I wasn't busy. . ."

He listened and laughed. "You know I was just thinking the same thing. Why don't we have the cookout here? I'll even provide the steaks!" He grinned, thinking of all the fresh meat he had in his bathtub. "Awesome! Saturday it is. Tell Dave it's his turn to bring the beer!" With another laugh, he hung up, shaking his head.

Mitch got the beer he wanted, grabbed a couple of boxes of gallon and quart freezer bags from a cabinet, and headed back to the bathroom. Setting everything down, he opened the beer and downed it. Tossing the bottle in the trashcan, he looked over the dark red masses of meat before him. Turning on the water in the tub, he picked up piece after piece, rinsing and then slicing them into the cuts he wanted before putting them into freezer bags. Before he knew it the meat was gone and he'd finished off one box of the quart bags and more than half of a box of gallon bags.

He set the steaks for the cookout aside so they wouldn't get mixed in with everything else. Gathering as much as he could in one armload, he headed out to his small garage to deposit the meat in his chest style deep freezer. He returned to the bathroom and did the same with the rest and put the steaks in the fridge in the house.

After washing out the tub and cleaning his knives with bleach, he took another quick shower. As he pulled on a pair of boxer shorts, his stomach rumbled and he remembered he hadn't eaten much for supper because he'd been disgusted by the woman and because he was looking forward to eating her later.

Wearing a grin as he walked to the kitchen, he opened the fridge, took out a bag which held one 'Marcy steak' and another beer. He set them on the counter and he grabbed a pair of tongs from a hook above the stove. Just the thought of a grilled steak had his mouth watering and his stomach growling louder in its eagerness. He was glad he'd purchased a gas grill when he'd moved in. He'd had a charcoal grill before and really liked the flavor they gave food, but the gas grill didn't take hours to heat up, so he'd decided to try it and was pleased with the ease of grilling it gave him. Collecting his food, beverage, utensil, and some seasoning, he once again headed out the back door, this time, not leaving the porch.

In minutes the grill was hot enough to start cooking. Opening the plastic bag, he used the tongs to fish out the raw, red meat. He half-laid it on top of the bag and sprinkled both sides with seasoning before he placed it on the hot grill; it sizzled and spit as the heat attacked the bloody liquid dripping from it. He shut the lid and let the heat do its job while he enjoyed his beer, standing on his porch in nothing but boxers, enjoying the peaceful night. A couple minutes passed before he opened the grill and flipped the steak – his stomach growling again as the aroma of it cooking rose into the air to tease him. Licking his lips, he reluctantly closed the grill again and took the bloody bag into the house and retrieved a plate. By the time he returned the steak was done to his liking. He turned off the grill and plated his prize with the tongs and went back inside.

After acquiring a steak knife, fork, and another beer from the kitchen when he put the tongs in the sink, he settled into his recliner to enjoy his meat. He cut into it slowly, watching the natural juices seep out and onto his plate. Raising the fork to his lips with the first bite impaled on its prongs, he paused for a moment, building anticipation for his tongue as he breathed in the intoxicating aroma of grilled human flesh. Placing the little chunk of meat in his mouth, he closed his lips over the fork, sliding the morsel off with his teeth as the flavor exploded on his tongue and he moaned in ecstasy. He savored each and every bite with his eyes closed as he lovingly chewed each piece before swallowing it. He ate more than half of the steak before taking a drink of his beer because he didn't want it to interrupt the circus of delight his mouth was experiencing.

Before he knew it, his steak was gone. His stomach was full, but he was still disappointed his enjoyment had to end. Putting his dishes in the sink, he made his way to bed, tired and sated from his meal.

Climbing into bed, he smiled, thinking about Saturday and the steaks waiting in the fridge. That thought alone kept him smiling even after he'd fallen asleep.

~ * ~

Saturday arrived and so did the band and their families. Mitch stood on his porch, proudly manning his grill while he watched the children playing in his yard, and the adults sitting or standing around talking; everyone wore happy smiles as they enjoyed themselves.

"Those steaks sure do smell good!" Dave said, coming up behind him and punching him lightly on the shoulder. "I wish you would tell me where you get your meat so I could go to the same butcher! Nothing I buy ever tastes the same."

Mitch laughed. "I would tell you, but then I'd have to kill ya!"

Dave laughed. "Fine, keep your secrets! You'll just have to cook for me more often that way, and I won't complain about that!"

"No," Mitch said, "I don't suppose you would. Hey, the meat's done – you want to get everyone rounded up so we can eat?"

"Sure thing, man," Dave said, heading down the steps and into Mitch's back yard to do just that.

Mitch removed all the meat from the grill – steaks for the adults and burgers for the kids – and put it on a large platter. He turned off the grill and headed down the steps himself, to the picnic tables setting off to the left side of his yard.

"Here you go!" he said, setting the plate in the middle of the table. "Enjoy!"

Everyone dug in and soon the heaping mound of meat was reduced to a few pieces to be saved for later.

"Hey, Mitch," Craig called from the far end of the table, "too bad you didn't invite that little blonde who has been stalking you, then you would've had a date for this party!"

Mitch laughed, eating the last bite of his steak. "Oh, she's here in spirit, I'm sure."

Craig laughed, and as Mitch looked around the table he saw that Troy had a smirk on his face. He winked at Mitch and shoved another bite of steak into his mouth.

She was there all right, and she was now a part of all of them. . .

HOPE OF A FUTURE

Everything started when H1N1 broke out. What some called the Swine Flu, which they had to change to appease the pork producers. Made sense, too – the pigs didn't have anything to do with it, so why scare people away from their beloved sausage and pork chops?

Most people had gotten the vaccine. I hadn't. I didn't want that stuff floating around in my system. All the hype only aggravated me. There were too many variables; they could have tested it more before they told everyone to get it.

You could have said I was paranoid, but, as it turns out, I was right. Of course no one knew for a few years, until whatever was in it latched onto DNA and babies were born deformed and with immunity diseases.

Even the effects of the vaccine were slow to be acknowledged because of the natural disasters. The memory of hurricane Katrina was starting to fade when the earthquakes started. Haiti, Chile. . .and then Japan. The nuclear plant disaster wasn't even that big of a deal at the end of the day. Humanity was screwed, after all, what did one more poisoning of resources and DNA mean, really?

They were strong quakes that left humanity reeling at our pitifully small existence in the great and unpredictable universe. Buildings and lives ripped apart, for what? Nature was contaminated, why? There was no reason. Earth decided to move and we suffered.

More quakes broke out until it was clear they weren't going to stop, that things weren't going to get better. All leading up to the volcanos.

As the quakes moved the plates underneath us, they shifted in ways that affected volcanic activity. Yellow Stone was the first to let us know what we were in for. A couple of small islands had formed in various parts of the ocean and live volcanos were showing activity, which was to be expected. But when Yellow Stone National Park blew up in a spewing froth of hot, searing magma, the future of the human race started to become clear.

We couldn't fight against anything so strong. How do you battle a planet that didn't want to play fair?

One after another, active and inactive volcanos erupted all over the world. The ash was terrible and unbearable; it covered the world for months.

Food shortages ensued. Thousands died. The end of the year 2017 was a nightmare. Not only the volcanic activity, but something else it triggered. It was bad enough that global warming had caused the ocean temperatures to rise, but the lava heated it even more. Tropical storms became a daily occurrence. Pretty soon hurricanes were hitting all the coast lines. They got stronger and stronger and all coastal cities were flooded.

They evacuated New York in time to save half the population. I can't even tell you how many people drowned in the subways. Sydney was wiped out as well. Not to mention England, Ireland – basically most of the coastal Europe was gone. Islands had disappeared and as far as anyone knew, no one had survived.

New Year's Day 2018 brought a whole new perspective on things when it came in with a bang. Who knew there was a dormant volcano under the glaciers? I don't think anyone did. I'm not even sure there was one there to begin with. I think that the heat under the surface of Earth was too much to be contained.

The splendid scene the red magma created as it shot up through white ice – sizzling and setting off explosions – would have been majestic if it hadn't been disastrous. Ice melted at a tremendous rate, again changing the temperature of the oceans.

Hurricanes became those things I watched a show about, on one of those educational channels, years ago: Hypercanes. The five-hundred mile per hour wind giants, with their ten-mile wide and twenty-mile high radius, poisoned plant and sea life; they reached all the way up to the ozone layer and laced the water with radiation. That's when everyone still alive was treated for radiation. We took pills and did everything we were told and was possible to try and keep ourselves from being poisoned to death. I think it was some vain attempt at repopulation – we couldn't produce healthy children if we were already tainted. I guess the scientists were trying to salvage what they could of a population for the future.

What was left of the coastal cities was flattened as the Hypercanes swept across continents; sometimes they would make it a good ways inland before fizzling out. Whole strips were torn out of countries, leaving nothing in their wake.

I heard one scientist say that the cause of all of the destruction and mayhem was the shifting of Earth's poles, starting in the year 2012 when the end of the world was supposed to have taken place. The celestial crosses met in the sky and started more than anyone ever dreamed of. It took years before the full effect showed its ugly face, but no one could have predicted it.

I figured we'd all be dead by now – I wasn't even sure Earth would survive this long. It seemed bound and determined to destroy itself as it wiped out our existence.

Still, despite it all, a few of us survived. The band I'm with now consists of twenty people: fourteen women and six men. We lived in a bunker, underground, to stay alive. It was small and tight, and we didn't get to go outside because of the radiation.

Somewhat safe in the bunker, we were dreading what might happen in the world beyond our reach. We didn't know how things could get any worse, but we'd thought that before and look where it'd gotten us. I didn't know what more could happen, unless the Earth spun off its orbit, and then it wouldn't matter anymore.

Days passed slowly, with nothing new happening, at least not that we knew about. Since all the satellites were out and we no longer had any kind of communication system to tell us what was going on in the world, we didn't know for sure. Something could have happened on the other side of the planet and we would never know.

All we know right now is that we're still alive and have to press on to revive humanity, if we can. The future is as uncertain as it has ever been, there are just fewer of us to live it. . .

~ * ~

"Brian, are you going to sit on your butt and write in that thing all day?" a feminine voice grumbled as a shadow fell over me.

I looked up to see Diane and I inwardly groaned.

"I was taking a short break," I said and stood, brushing dirt from the seat of my pants. "We're allowed to have breaks you know."

"Short breaks are allowed, yes, but not every ten minutes."

I itched to tell her that she knew I didn't take breaks every ten minutes, like she did, but I held my tongue. Life was hard enough without adding more conflict, not that Diane thought about that when she was bossing people around.

I saw Kate glance our way and raise an eyebrow. I shut my journal and tucked it into my back pocket, along with my pen. Smiling defiantly at Diane, I stepped past her and joined the other two in our work group, who were searching the wreckage for food and anything else we could use.

Thankfully the radiation hadn't been that bad in our area. We were also lucky enough to have a scientist in our band. Otherwise, we wouldn't have known if it'd been safe to venture out of the bunker. Harry was traveling with two others to see how far we could go in each direction and in essence, setting up a parameter. Once that was complete, we could do a better job searching for supplies.

Kate smiled as I helped her lift a heavy piece of sheet metal she was struggling with.

"Did you get in trouble?" Kate teased.

"Yeah," I said. "Diane is in a mood today."

Kate laughed. "She's in a mood every day. Why would today be any different?"

I snickered. "True. Did I miss anything major?"

"No," Kate said. "I think there might be enough sheet metal around to build a shelter, but other than that, no great finds."

We added the metal to the pile of useful things we'd found. I stood and looked around, taking in the landscape, hoping to spot something we'd missed. I couldn't help but notice Diane was now taking a break; it was her third one today. She took more breaks than anyone else and still complained when we took ours.

Shaking my head, I followed Kate to another piece of sheet metal. Heather joined us.

"I found a couple cans that might be food," Heather announced. "The labels are missing, so I don't know what's in them."

"That's better than nothing," I said. "With that and the building supplies, we should have a good bit to take back with us. We might even have to make more than one trip."

Heather nodded. "At least we'll have something to show for the day. It seems more often than not, we don't find anything of use or value."

Kate and I added another sheet to the stack and the three of us walked up the hill. We paused at the top and surveyed, not for the first time, the devastation of our world.

Few trees could be seen, and those which did remain were mere skeletons of what they'd once been. The ground was bare of any and all vegetation. The endless swath of brown dirt was littered with scraps of trash and occasionally a car or truck mangled so badly as to be almost unrecognizable.

We'd been sent north today. Each day a group was assigned a different direction. Yesterday we'd been sent southeast. It gave us a chance to see what was around us, as well as have new sets of eyes on areas where something might have been missed by others. There was so much to dig through that we could only get a small area searched in one day.

Kate sighed. "I still don't know how we survived."

"Me neither," Heather added.

I didn't have anything to say. Everything was gone and I still couldn't get my mind around it.

"What are you three doing?" Diane huffed as she mounted the rise to stand on the other side of Heather. "Standing here isn't getting any work done."

I glanced at Kate and saw her jaw tense.

"I think it's time for Heather's break," I said, waiting for Diane to say something snippy.

Diane kept her mouth shut for once.

Heather turned toward me, smiled, and winked as she made her way back down the hill to take a break.

"I think we have enough for today," Diane said, looking at our piles. "We should head back now."

Kate clenched her fists and closed her eyes; I could see she was battling for control.

"I think it's early," I said. "We've just had breaks. We can get those piles doubled, if not tripled, before the day's out."

"Who are you to say if we have enough?" Diane asked. "You're not the boss."

"No," Kate snapped. "I am, and I think we can get a lot more work in today."

Diane looked down at the ground, her face beet red. Kate didn't usually exert her authority over our search party and I think it caught Diane by surprise. I did my best not to grin.

"We're going to start over there and everyone is going to help," Kate said. "Heather will join us after her break, and then I'll take one. After that, unless we have to lift something heavy or do something else that's tasking, there will be no more breaks."

I tried to smother a laugh, but snorted from the effort. Without looking at either of them I made my way down the far side of the hill and started working where Kate had indicated.

A few moments later I heard the shifting and scraping of shoes on dry ground as they joined me. Together we lifted a fairly large chunk of cement to see what was under it. There was a cabinet, half of a porcelain kitchen sink, and some scraps of cloth; after setting the cement aside we investigated our findings.

Kate gripped the handles on the doors of what looked to be a solid wood cabinet for a garage or pantry, and glanced up at us.

Diane and I nodded in unison as we held our breaths.

I was hoping the cabinet was from a pantry and that the back, which was facing the ground, wasn't missing and there was actually something useful, like food, inside.

"What did you find?" Heather called from the hill above us.

We all jumped at the sound of her voice.

"We don't know yet," Kate hollered back. "Might be something. Might be nothing."

"Wait for me," Heather yelled, and rushed down the hill.

Heather was one of the youngest of the survivors at seventeen and was often impetuous. It was nice. When she was around, we weren't surrounded by gloom all the time, which almost made up for having to deal with Diane, almost, but not quite.

Kate resumed her grip on the handles and this time didn't wait; she tugged on the doors.

They didn't budge.

We all sighed in unison. The tension was thick. We were running out of food and drinkable water. If there was food in the cabinet, we needed it badly.

"I'll help," I said. "Maybe it's just stuck."

Stepping forward I gripped one of the handles with both hands; Kate did the same with the other.

"One," Kate said. "Two. Three!"

We jerked as hard as we could and the door gave way. The four of us peered inside. There was nothing in the cabinet. As I'd feared, the back was missing and everything that had once been contained within was gone.

I bowed my head and leaned forward with my hands on my knees. After a couple of deep breaths, I stood. Everyone's face mirrored my disappointment.

"The cabinet is in good condition," I said, trying to look on the bright side. "We can use it for something. I'm sure we can fashion a new back for it."

I pretended not to see the tears in Kate's dark brown eyes as she nodded and looked off into the distance.

"Help me lift this so we can see if there's anything under it," I said to the other two, drawing their attention away from Kate.

It took all three of us to lift it; the cabinet was old, probably an antique, otherwise, I don't think it would have made it in such good condition. We stood it on a fairly level spot at the base of the hill.

By the time we walked back over Kate had herself under control and was attempting to move the broken sink by herself. Heather made it to her side in time to help her before she dropped the sharp end on her foot; together they tossed it over the cement chunk.

We worked together to remove some layers of house siding and insulation; it took a while. It appeared that a whole bunch of stuff had landed here, probably deposited by a Hypercane, filling in a deep depression in the ground. Everything was packed so tightly we had to pry it out with sticks and anything else we could find for leverage. After an hour of hard labor we all wanted to sit down. The air, lacking normal levels of oxygen because of the vegetation shortage, plus exertion, worked against us.

I glanced at Kate and raised an eyebrow. She shrugged.

"Let's all take a break," Kate said. "We've been working harder than I thought we'd have to."

Diane grumbled something under her breath and wandered off to find somewhere to sit.

"You never did take your break earlier, did you?" I asked Kate as we sat together in the shade of the hill.

She shook her head and lay back, closing her eyes.

Heather wandered back over the hill, I assumed to get a drink of water. I silently hoped she'd bring some back with her. Knowing her thoughtful nature I didn't doubt that she would.

Lying beside Kate, I reached over and took her hand in mine. She squeezed and smiled.

Kate and I were close to the same age. I was thirty-four and she was thirty-two. We'd bonded instantly. I couldn't help but be attracted to her. She was sweet, kind, strong, and beautiful.

It was dangerous to fall in love and we both knew it. Because of the number of men versus women who'd survived, relationships would be difficult, if not destructive. Our band had decided collectively that the best way to rebuild the human race would be through an emotion free breeding program of sorts. The men would try to get all the women pregnant. It was more structured, but that's what it melted down to. There was also no way of knowing if any of them were sterile, so it improved the odds of pregnancies among the women.

Kate knew the risk and so did I. We just couldn't seem to help how we felt about each other.

I squeezed her hand and rubbed the back of her knuckles with my thumb.

"I'm sorry the cabinet was empty."

She sighed deeply. "It's frustrating. We're eking by day to day on almost nothing. I sometimes think we would've been better off if we hadn't survived."

"Yes," I said. "Maybe we would have."

"I brought some water for you guys," Heather announced, coming back over the hill waving a bottle of water.

Kate discretely withdrew her hand from mine and stood. "Great. It's time to get back to work anyway."

Kate took the bottle from Heather and downed half of it, handing the rest to me.

"Did you bring some for Diane?" Kate asked.
Heather nodded.
"Would you tell her break's over?"

"Sure," Heather said as she headed in the direction of Diane's disappearance.

We started where we'd left off, and it wasn't long before Heather and Diane joined us. We moved quickly and with renewed energy. It helped that we knew when we finished we'd be heading back to camp for the day.

We'd been rummaging and moving things for quite a while when we hit something solid. I thought it might be a rock and that we'd finally found the bottom of the pile. After clearing everything away I found out I was wrong. It was a board, about the size of a door, and it was wedged into the dirt at an angle. It took all four of us to pull it out, and when we saw what was laying underneath it we froze.

There, lying in the bottom of the pit was a mound of canned food.

Kate fell to her knees, staring at it, like she couldn't believe what she was seeing.

I grinned like an idiot.

Heather laughed. "Food! I can't believe we found food! I mean, I hoped, but I never expected to actually find some."

Diane didn't say anything. She, like Kate, seemed to be in a state of shocked disbelief.

"How are we going to carry it all?" I asked absently, looking around for something that would hold the food.

Kate looked up at me and blinked. "What? Oh, I think we could probably use the board that was covering it. We can stack it on there and each of us can support a corner."

That's how we ended up arriving back at camp. All of us carrying the door sized board – which was actually the back of the cabinet – covered with food and other useful stuff we'd found.

Everyone ran out into the dusky evening to greet us, as we were the last to return. They cheered when they saw what we'd found.

Marcus stepped forward and raised his hands to quiet the excited group of people before he spoke.

"I would like to thank Kate, Diane, Brian, and Heather for finding food. It'll go a long way in keeping us alive. This food, along with the water Steve, Marie, Tony, and Patty found, should last for a while."

Everyone cheered again.

We took the food over to the cooking area. A couple of people helped us unload and stack the cans, a few prized bottles of juice, and everything else we'd found.

Finally, we sat down by the communal fire and were given something to eat. Normally no one was waited on, but since we'd gotten back late and were kind of heroes for the day, it was allowed.

I saw Marcus sit beside Kate and I tried not to get jealous. Marcus was our voted leader. He was smart and muscular with dark, wavy hair and hazel eyes. I'd seen every woman in camp looking at him at one time or another. I figured they were all waiting for the breeding process to begin. It wasn't really called the breeding process, it was called repopulation, but it all boiled down to breeding and I knew most of the women couldn't wait for their turn with him.

Kate laughed at something he said and I knew I had to get away before I did something stupid.

Gulping down the rest of my meager meal and quickly washing my bowl, I made my way out of camp. I pulled my journal out of my back pocket as I trudged off into the darkness. I didn't know how much I could write in the dark, but I knew it would keep my mind occupied and off of subjects that would get me into trouble.

~ * ~

Thankfully, the bunker we'd found and hid in had a store of food, water, and drugs to help our bodies survive and resist the radiation. It kept us alive for a long time. From the marks we'd made on the walls, it looked to be a grand total of two years we'd lived underground.

Harry, the scientist, warned us about radiation from the Hypercanes. The knowledge that we could die if we went outside too soon kept us somewhat content underground. He'd found a radiation suit and some detection gear stashed inside a yellow suitcase and we made good use of it.

After the first year, he'd send one of us at a time to the surface to check the radiation levels. Although we didn't get a reading on the meter for the last six months, we still stayed underground. Don't ask me why. I think we were all afraid of what we'd find on the surface, or what we wouldn't find.

Harry and Marcus decided we should stay where we were for a while, just in case the meter was wrong. If it was right, then we wouldn't have anything to worry about, but they didn't know if we were the only ones to survive and I guess we just couldn't risk it.

By the time they let us out we were ready to strangle each other, but that would have been breaking the law. That's what we did, while we were down there, we made laws. I guess we had to have some structure to follow.

We didn't make too many laws, at least not too many major ones. You weren't allowed to willfully do anything to hurt another person, which included killing. You also had to do your best to keep peace; if you started a fight with someone you would get in serious trouble. I don't know exactly what the serious trouble would be because it's not like you would be killed for any offense, after all, we were the last people on Earth as far as we knew. . .

After we 'declared' most of the laws, it was agreed that we needed to come up with a strategy to continue the human race, what I think of as the 'breeding program.'

Since there are more than twice as many women as there are men, it was decided that there would be a system put in place. Each man would spend one week with the women, sleeping with as many different ones as he could, and then have a night to rest before going back to work. Then the next man would do the same thing, until they all had a turn. Once a woman was pregnant, she would be taken out of the rotation. Once all the women were pregnant, they'd be more careful and the men would do more of the work.

We all agreed to the plan, but we also agreed we needed to get on the surface to see what we were dealing with before anyone got pregnant. That way, the women could help with the work, until we had shelter and were stable.

The work wasn't broken up into male work and female work, it was just work. You took care of yourself and you did what duties were assigned to you and your work crew.

That was how it came about that I was spending more time with Kate. She's my crew leader. We'd taken to each other right away, but I really don't know what she sees in me. I'm somewhat tall and slimly built. I have flat wiry muscles and plain brown hair. My eyes are light gray and there's nothing unique about me.

Maybe it's my sparkling personality and wit, but I doubt it. . .

~ * ~

"Brian?"

I jumped as someone said my name from close-by. "Who is it?"

A soft feminine laugh floated to me on the evening breeze.

"Kate?"

"Yes," Kate said as she stepped into my line of vision. "What are you doing out here all by yourself?"

I laughed. "What are you doing looking for me out here all by yourself?"

Kate sat beside me, grinning. "I thought something was wrong when you took off. Wanna talk about it?"

Looking down at my journal, I sighed. "No, I don't think so."

"Oh, come on," Kate teased, and bumped her shoulder against mine. "Tell me. Maybe I can help."

Glancing sideways at Kate I decided to take my chances.

"I think I'm in love with you," I said quietly.

Kate didn't reply.

I turned toward her and watched her as I continued. "If it wasn't for all of this," I swung my arm up and gestured at the world around us, "I would be dating you, hoping that someday we'd be married and have children together. But, because of where we are, and what life has dealt, I'll have to pretend it doesn't bother me when I have to share you with other men."

Kate's eyes welled up with tears. They fell as she looked down at her hands, which were clenched together in her lap.

"Brian," she whispered, "I love you, too. But we can't act on our feelings. It would hurt us all."

I don't know what I expected, but hearing her say she loved me too overwhelmed me with a joyous hope. I took her hands in mine.

"Please," I begged, "stay with me tonight. Be with me tonight. No one has to know. I love you so much."

Kate took a shuddering breath. "No."

She ripped her hands from mine, stood, and fled back toward camp.

My heart fell. Where there was joy and hope moments ago, there was now a burning weight that made it hard for me to breathe. How could she say she loved me and then refuse to share that love with me? I was devastated. Anger sizzled through my body in the form of adrenaline.

I wanted to break something, to kill something, to tear everything apart. I felt that if I could make everything and everyone around me hurt as much as I was hurting then the pain would cease.

Mostly I hated myself for telling Kate that I loved her.

Thoughts of things I could do to myself, of things that would end my life, flashed through my head. They teased my soul with the promise of release. Images of knives sinking into my flesh and other twisted dark ideas taunted me.

Mentally shaking myself, I dragged my hands through my hair in torment and frustration. Through a force of will I dispelled the temptations from my mind. I couldn't hurt myself. I couldn't allow things to drive me to that. If I did, I would never see Kate again. Maybe I could change her mind, make her see that it was right for us to be together.

With that thought, the thought of a maybe in the future, a calm settled over me. A cold shaft of resolve stole through me, turning my anger and hurt into determination.

Standing, I turned toward camp and put one foot in front of the other as a plan began to form in my brain, a plan to win Kate for myself.

~ * ~

The next day dawned hot and muggy. I hadn't slept well, even though I'd been exhausted. My plan was swirling in my head and it wouldn't let me rest.

Getting ready to go out and get to work, I continued to think of ways I could make things right – the way they should be, instead of the way they were – while mentally preparing myself for any obstacles that might get in my way ahead of time so I could handle them effectively. But an unexpected obstacle reared its ugly head nonetheless. I was switched to another work crew.

As Marcus announced the change, I glanced to my right where Kate was standing. She stared straight ahead. I had a sneaking suspicion she'd asked for me to be moved to another crew. A suspicion that was given more strength when I saw Marcus give her a barely perceptible nod.

At that moment I hated Marcus for coming between Kate and me. My jealousy made me think he just wanted her for himself and she'd been toying with me and really wanted to be with him.

I clenched my fists and jaw. Closing my eyes, I took deep, steadying breaths. I felt betrayed and used.

They'll pay for this, I thought to myself as I almost passed out from the intensity of the feelings swirling within me.

"Brian, are you all right?"

I opened my eyes and consciously relaxed my tense muscles. "Yes, Heather, I'm fine."

"I can't believe they moved you to another crew," Heather said. "We all work so well together, as well as we can anyway, with Diane around. I'm going to miss you."

"I know," I said – I couldn't think of anything else to tell her. She didn't need to be brought into everything that was going on. "It'll be all right. Jesse is nice. You shouldn't have any trouble getting along."

"It won't be the same," Heather said, and pouted in her young, innocent way. "I like you and wish you were still going to work with us. Maybe you can talk to Kate and see if they'll switch you back."

I shook my head grimly. "No. We'll just go with the changes. I'm sure there's a reason for them."

I turned and walked away, heading toward my new group before Heather could say anything else – I already had enough going on in my head without her unknowingly adding more.

I inwardly fumed all day about being shoved off without any thoughts about my feelings. Although everyone was nice and we all worked well together, it just wasn't the same. I missed Kate, and I hated her because I missed her. I knew better, but my mind insisted she'd done this on purpose to hurt me. While in my heart I knew she'd done it to keep us both from doing something stupid that we'd regret later.

When we got back to camp that night, I looked for Kate among the others; they hadn't returned yet.

Applying myself to help build a permanent shelter for us to live in, I let my mind wander. I thought about what it would have been like if I'd met Kate before the *Wrath of Earth,* as we all called it. In my mind we were happy, we got married, and had healthy, beautiful children.

My thoughts were still in a wonderland of what-ifs when Kate, Heather, Diane, and Jesse returned.

After a supper of rice and kidney beans, I set off by myself again, going to the same place as the night before, thinking that maybe if I wrote about the past, something of the future might become clear to me.

I settled down and withdrew my leather journal from my pocket, smoothing my hand over its cracked, worn surface, not knowing if anyone would ever read it and wondered if I was wasting my time. In reality, it didn't matter. I needed the outlet. I had to have something to give me purpose.

Opening to where I'd left off last night, I stared off into the distance, watching the sun slowly set behind the barren hills in the distance. As orange and red rays bathed the desolate landscape a movement caught my attention.

I paused with my pen floating above my journal. *Is someone out wandering around in the dark?*

As I watched, a man stepped over the rise, silhouetted in the purple dusk of last light. He was bigger than anyone I'd seen in a long time and was carrying a rifle.

Slowly – careful not to draw attention to myself – I stood and put my journal away. I stepped back and squatted in the shadow of the boulder I'd been leaning against. I watched as another man, who also had a gun, joined the first.

They talked to each other briefly, one gesturing behind them, the other motioning toward the east and our settlement. After their exchange the second man made a motion and a small cluster of people joined them. I couldn't tell how many there were or their gender, I could only see that they were armed. They had guns, pitchforks, swords, and I don't know what else.

I knew I had to get back to camp and warn everyone.

Slinking through the darkness, I was glad I was tall and slender, making it easier for me to move quietly.

After I was sure I was far enough away that they wouldn't see me, I started to run. My lungs burned from the effort, but I couldn't slow down. I didn't want to think about what would happen if I didn't get there in time to warn everyone.

I slid to a halt just inches from the fire, too winded to talk for at least a minute; by the time I caught my breath everyone had gathered and was watching me anxiously.

"I saw a group of people," I said, still gulping for air.

"People!" I heard someone call out in excitement.

"We aren't the only ones alive!" Someone else said.

I held up my hand and took a deep breath before speaking. "They're armed with guns. They look well too – the one man I saw was huge. They have to be eating better than we are."

Marcus stepped forward. "If that's true and they mean us harm then they could easily overpower us. Were they all men, Brian? How many of them are there?"

I shook my head. "Most of them looked male, but they were too far away to tell. I didn't get a count either, there might be fifteen, twenty, probably more."

Everyone was silent as they listened. The first voice I heard was in a way, expected.

"We don't know if they're going to try to hurt us," Diane said. "They could just be travelers in search of other people. Maybe they ran out of food or something where they were."

I shook my head and glanced at Marcus; he was deep in thought and hadn't heard Diane.

Since no one said anything to oppose her, she kept going.

"I think we should send a small group out to meet them and talk," Diane said louder, getting drunk on the attention. "I think it would be in our best interest to see if they come in peace."

"No," Marcus said.

"That's what we'll do," Diane continued. "We'll meet with them and see what they want."

"No," Marcus said forcefully. "We aren't going to do that. We can't risk getting hurt."

"What are we going to do?" Diane asked sarcastically, with her hands on her hips and her head swaying with attitude. "Hide like rabbits in a hole and wait for them to leave?"

"We're going to arm ourselves and defend our home," Marcus said.

Heads turned toward Marcus and back to Diane. I could see everyone's minds calculating the difference in the plans. I could see our community splitting and taking sides.

Murmurs vibrated into the night air. Some agreed with Diane and stepped closer to her, lending their support with suggestions and volunteering to go with her. Others remained with Marcus and asked what he had in mind. I put my trust in Marcus. Caution was the best policy for survival.

Marcus tried one last time to convince Diane that her plan was dangerous. "Please Diane, don't do this. If you're wrong and they're intent on harm, you could be killed. Think of it this way, at least staying together as one force, we might have a chance if they're hostile."

Diane rolled her eyes, turned her back on Marcus, and stomped away.

Marcus sighed and shook his head.

Glancing at those of us who were left – those of us prepared to fight – I counted a total of twelve. Diane had only convinced four people. That was a small number, but they were people we could have used. The dozen of us quickly discussed and formed a plan.

We had no guns, they had that advantage over us, but we did have an array of weaponry at our disposal. Before the world turned into a living hell, I'd been quite good at archery. Trees were limited, but I'd managed to find enough wood to make three long bows and some arrows; I'd been training a couple of the others to use them. We'd mostly planned on using them for hunting, but defense was just as good and had always been another likely possibility.

I took one myself and gave one to Tony, who'd been doing well with the lessons. I looked around for Jesse, who'd been my star pupil, and realized that he'd gone with Diane. I gave the last one to Heather; she lacked the strength for long shots, but up close she was extremely accurate.

Marcus and Steve had fashioned machetes out of some metal we'd found – they would work for swords. The weapons weren't very well balanced or graceful, but they were sharp. Those, added to two axes we'd found, armed us all.

The archers were to go outside of the camp and hide. Marcus would wait by the fire to meet the horde when they arrived, while the rest were to hide where they could easily attack from different angles.

I perched on the top of a large chunk of sandstone above our settlement. I could see Diane and her followers walking out toward where I'd seen the people; they carried three torches and were easy to spot.

They hadn't gone far when a group of four or five men met them. They stood and talked for a few minutes. I saw one of them punch Diane in the face. In a blink the five people who'd gone out to offer peace were surrounded. Jesse fought, but to no avail. A loud *boom* resounded through the emptiness as he was shot.

I was stricken as I watched Jesse's body fall and the strangers commenced with beating the rest of them into submission.

I looked down and saw Marcus rise to his feet. He walked to the west side of the fire with his sword in hand, waiting.

I stood and got ready. Since we now knew they were hostile, we were allowed to shoot as soon as we had a good target.

I nocked an arrow and drew back on the string of my bow. The fletching tickled my fingers as I waited at full draw. I knew I had to make every arrow count since we only had ten each.

They had Diane, and her followers, tied up and gagged. I was shocked to see that Jesse's body was also in tow.

Why would they keep a dead man? I wondered to myself.

Marcus stood his ground and waited until they were twenty feet from him. "You're not welcome here. Release those of us you've captured and leave now. We don't wish to fight you; there's no need for more death."

The big man laughed and stepped forward. "I disagree. There *is* need for more death. We must eat and you, my friend, are meat."

That explains why they kept the dead body, I thought with a shudder. *They plan to eat it.*

Taking careful aim, I relaxed my hand and let the arrow fly. It struck the man in the eye; he fell, instantly dead. Blood spurted from the wound a good foot in the air while he lay there and everyone recovered from the initial surprise and shock of the swift attack.

"That's what will happen to the rest of you if you don't leave now," Marcus shouted, brandishing his sword.

A woman growled viciously and leaped at Marcus. He stepped aside and brought his sword down on the back of her neck. It sank into her flesh, chopping her head halfway off in a fountain of gushing blood; it coated Marcus and mixed with the fountain from the man's head.

I released another arrow as I saw many of them reach for their guns. It struck a man in the neck, shedding more blood. Other arrows were striking further back in the crowd; Tony and Heather were hitting their targets as well.

Marcus bellowed like a crazy man and charged those in the lead. He took down two before they even saw him coming. The six others of our band attacked the horde in the middle, three on each side. I saw the other two attack the rear.

They were well armed, but they'd taken for granted that their size and state of arm would frighten us into submitting. Either that or they'd thought we wouldn't be able to defend ourselves. Their miscalculation was serving us well.

I had three more arrows and I released them in quick succession, all of them flew true. After that, I left my perch to join the fray.

I slid down the hill and into the battle, slipping in blood and falling over a body in my rush. Retrieving a gun, I aimed at a man who was breaking away from the others. I squeezed the trigger and screamed in pain as the recoil assaulted my shoulder. I fell to my knees, almost passing out from pain. I saw that I'd shot him in the leg; he was on the ground trying to drag himself to safety.

Grinding my teeth, I forced myself to stand and advanced toward him. I dropped the gun and grabbed a dagger still in the clutches of a severed hand. Frustrated when a couple of shakes didn't dislodge it, I dropped the hand onto the ground and violently stomped on it until the fingers let loose. Bending to pick up the knife, I saw a movement to my right. Clutching the dagger in my left hand, I spun toward my foe. Thrusting upward I caught the advancing woman in the gut, slicing her all the way up to her cheek. She wailed like a banshee and stumbled back in dazed shock as her guts spilled out from her body with a sickening *squish*. I drew back and stabbed her in the throat, and as I ripped the blade back out, she collapsed. Seeing that she was finished completely and not getting back up, I returned my attention to the man I'd injured.

He was sitting up against a rock, holding a gun across his lap. I suspected by his labored breathing and the pool of blood underneath his leg that he was bleeding to death. A suspicion that was confirmed as I watched him take his last, gasping breath.

Screams of pain and yelling drew my attention back to what was going on around me. I surveyed the rest of the battle before rushing in to help a couple of women who were surrounded. The men who encroached upon them were so focused and intent that they didn't notice me. Upper-cutting at a sharp angle, I caught the largest of the men in the left side. I threw all my weight into the thrust, hoping I'd penetrate the short blade all the way to his heart.

All eyes turned toward me as the man cried out and fell. The women took the opportunity to kill one of the other men.

The third man stabbed at me with a knife of his own. I blocked the best I could, but fell over the head of someone who'd been decapitated, releasing the dagger that was buried to the hilt in the other man's ribs; the man managed to injure my good arm as I lost my footing. I groped around me for something to use to defend myself, finding an arm. I swung it upward in desperation. The arm whipped out straight, causing the hand to slap my attacker across the face. We both paused and looked at each other. If this hadn't been a life or death situation I would have laughed at the absurdity of what had just happened and the look of shock on his face.

I lifted the arm again as he raised his knife to strike, but a blade exploded from his chest in a bloom of bright red blood. I swung my arm up to protect my face as he fell, forgetting that I was still gripping the severed arm. It wrapped around the man's neck as he landed atop me, holding him to me as if I were drawing him close for a kiss.

I quickly released the arm in disgust and wriggled out from under him. Marcus stood over me holding his machete and breathing heavily. He was covered from head to toe in blood and human tissue.

"You all right, Brian?" he asked.

I nodded and struggled to my feet. "I think so."

"What happened to your arm? Did you get shot?"

"No," I said with a lopsided grin. "I didn't hold a rifle right when I fired it. I think I dislocated my shoulder."

We turned to view the slaughter ground. We'd managed to hold our own.

"Did we lose anyone?" I asked Marcus.

"I don't know yet," Marcus said. "You were the last one fighting. Let's go see how many made it to rendezvous point."

I nodded and followed him.

I was relieved to see Kate, Heather, and a good many others. Out of the twelve of us who'd chosen to fight, only two had been lost. While many had various injuries, everyone seemed to be all right. Diane and two of her followers were there as well.

Marcus sighed heavily. "I want everyone who's injured to get your wounds washed and treated. Anyone who's able, come help me clean up this mess."

After my shoulder was jerked back into place and the cut on my arm was bandaged, I went to help stack and burn the bodies. I made sure to recover the dagger from the corpse of the man I'd killed with it before he was added to the fire.

A short time later, Heather came running out to Marcus.

"It's all gone," Heather wailed. "There's nothing left. No food, no water. Nothing!"

"Damn it," Marcus growled. "Someone must have snuck in and taken everything while we were fighting. What about the emergency store?"

"Patty and Marie went to look," Heather said.

There was some talk about sending a search party out to see if we could catch whoever had taken our supplies, but we didn't know which direction they'd gone or how long ago they'd left.

Marie assured us later that the emergency rations were intact. It was good news that didn't cheer anyone up. The emergency store would only sustain us for a week.

~ * ~

Harry and his group returned a couple of days later. By that time we'd packed up and were ready to move to a new location. The stench of the shed blood was making us sick and drawing random animals, which in turn was a blessing – we killed them for their meat and their hides.

Harry said it was safe for us to travel north, so that's the way we went.

After we set up our tents that first night, I watched Kate across the fire, wondering how much longer we had to live. She still wouldn't talk to me or look at me. I knew we could die tonight, or tomorrow, or a week from now. All I could think about was being with her. I had nothing else to live for and I knew I had to take action if we were ever going to be together.

As darkness settled around us, I excused myself, pretending to be tired, but I didn't go to bed. Instead I circled out around camp to a spot where I could see what everyone was doing and waited.

Marcus and Kate were the last two at the fire. They sat for a long time, not saying anything. Marcus was the one who broke the silence, and in the calm, quiet night I could hear everything he said.

"Are you all right? I know the battle was hard on everyone, but you've been especially quiet."

Kate shrugged.

"Kate," Marcus said, "look at me, please."

She did, but she seemed reluctant.

"I know it was hard to kill people. It wasn't easy for any of us."

Kate shrugged again.

Marcus sighed. "I hate to see you this way."

"I'll be fine," Kate muttered. "Don't worry about me."

Marcus dragged a hand through his hair. "I can't help but worry. I care about you, Kate, more than I should."

Marcus reached over and took her hand in his.

"Marcus," Kate said, pulling her hand free. "No."

"We could die tonight, tomorrow, anytime! I can't keep my feelings inside any longer. This could be my only chance."

"I don't care for you that way," Kate said, standing. "I'm sorry, Marcus."

"Wait," Marcus said, standing as well.

"What?" Kate said turning toward him. "There's nothing more to say."

He reached up, cupped her face in his hands and kissed her.

I growled, wanting to tear him apart for touching her.

Kate pulled away and ran to her tent.

I sat silent and tense, waiting for Marcus to go to bed. He sat by himself for a half hour just gazing into the fire, before he finally turned in for the night.

I waited an additional half hour before I moved. Getting up slowly, I rubbed my legs to restore the circulation. Even though the night was chilly, I wasn't cold. I was buzzing with adrenaline and stored up emotion.

I moved through camp clutching the dagger I'd kept from the battle. It would serve me well.

As stealthy as a cat, I entering each tent methodically. I did what I had to do and left. It seemed like mere moments had passed when I found myself in front of Marcus'. I'd saved him for last, knowing he might have trouble sleeping after the touching scene by the fire.

I entered and paused. His steady breathing assured me he was asleep. I knelt beside him, pressed the dagger against his throat, and let it sink in. His eyes flew open and he gripped my arm as his warm blood ran across my hand. He was the only one who'd woken, the only one who'd looked into my eyes as I took their life.

"I've taken care of everyone," I whispered. "They won't suffer. I'll make sure Kate is happy."

Marcus gurgled as his grip went lax and his eyes lost their focus.

I felt at peace with myself, with the world. I knew everything was going to be all right now.

My steps were lighter as I made my way to Kate's tent. Slowly, I drew back the flap and crawled inside. Kate was lying on her stomach, facing away from me. I held my breath for a moment and just looked at her. From the top of her head down to her toes that were peeking out from under her blanket.

She'd drawn the covers up over her neck to ward of the cold. The only parts of her I could see were her toes, her dark hair, and the side of her face.

Leaning forward, I gently kissed her cheek and drew the blanket off of her shoulder, kissing her there as well; she stirred but didn't wake. I continued to remove her covers until they were lying around her ankles. I let my fingers trail up her calf, and pressed my palm against her warm, soft thigh as I slid my hand up her body.

Kate made a soft moaning sound in her sleep as I cupped her bottom, squeezing it gently before going higher. When I reached around to cup her breast she gasped and half-turned in my direction.

"Brian?" she asked in a dreamy voice.

"Yes, my darling, it's me," I said as I leaned forward and traced her lips with my tongue.

She opened her lips for me with a gasp, wrapping her arm around my neck.

I kissed her deeply as she turned over and pressed a hand against my chest.

She froze and pulled back. "What's all over you? Why are you wet and sticky?"

"It was necessary, my love, so we can be together as we should be," I said, reaching forward to caress her shoulders. "I cleared the path for our happiness. I saved them all from more torture in the process."

"Saved who?" Kate asked, shoving my hands away and sitting up. "What're you talking about? What've you done, Brian?"

"I killed them all. I slit their throats while they were sleeping. They won't suffer through starvation and dehydration. Best of all, we can be together. There's no one to stand in our way."

Kate gasped and slid further away from me, her eyes dropping to the dagger still clutched in my hand.

"Kate," I whispered. "It's all right. It had to be done. It's for the best."

"You're crazy," she said in a scared, shaky voice.

"It's okay," I said, reaching for her.

"No," Kate screamed, frantically trying to get away from me. "Don't touch me!"

Dropping the dagger, I grabbed her ankles and flipped her over onto her back as she tried to crawl out of the tent. Straddling her, I pinned her arms above her head, pressing her struggling body down with the weight of mine.

"You're covered in blood," Kate chocked out, and tried to twist herself free.

"I'm sorry," I snapped. "I know you're upset right now, but if you'd just calm down and think about it, you'd see that I did the right thing."

Kate whimpered and frantically tried to tug her wrists from my grasp.

"Calm down," I growled, squeezing tighter. "I don't want to hurt you."

She stopped struggling and looked up at me with tears in her eyes. "Please, Brian, don't hurt me. Let me go."

I stared down at her for a moment. "If I let you go, do you promise to calm down?"

She stifled a sob and nodded.

I released her as I gently kissed her shaking lips.

Kate reached up and wrapped an arm around my neck, kissing me back. I moaned and thrust my hands into her hair, relaxing my body on top of hers.

A moment later I felt a sharp, hot pain under my left shoulder blade. I reared back and cried out. Kate brought her knee up hard against my groin, wrenched herself free, and scrambled out of the tent.

Twisting, I saw the dagger that I'd carelessly dropped sticking out of my back.

Roaring in frustration and agony, I reached over my shoulder and ripped the knife out. Diving out of the tent, I spun around to see where she'd gone. I spotted her running toward a gulch to the south. Ignoring the pain in my crotch, I forced myself from a hobble to a run as I gave chase.

I felt betrayed and angry with her for turning on me. I'd done all of this for her, for our love, and she'd thrown my gift in my face.

Grinning, I realized I was gaining on her. She stumbled and fell when she glanced back over her shoulder to check my progress. In just moments I stood over her, panting. I held the knife at my side and just looked down at her.

She was selfish and ungrateful. She wasn't the woman I thought she was, the woman I loved.

Kate stared up at me, her eyes wild. "Please, Brian, don't. . ."

I raised the blade, and with all my strength and weight, plunged it through her heart. I knelt there beside her as she died, with my head bowed, my eyes closed, and my hands gripping the hilt of the dagger.

My eyelids glowed red. I opened them to see the sun bathing the earth with the first rays of morning sunshine.

Standing, I left the knife where it was, piercing Kate's heart. I turned and went back to camp, weaving with exhaustion and blood loss. The world spun around me. Vertigo made my stomach lurch. I fell down on my hands and knees and crawled back into Kate's tent.

Fatigue was taking over. I knew I wouldn't be able to stay awake much longer. As fast as I could, I bunched up a shirt that was lying close-by and pressed it to my back. I rolled up one of Kate's blankets and tied it around myself, using it to hold the shirt on as a bandage.

I was so weak by the time I was done I could barely drag myself along the ground to Kate's pillow. That's where I passed out, with her scent surrounding me.

~ * ~

It was early afternoon when I woke up; I still felt weak and spaced out. The world seemed like a faraway dream that I was floating through.

I made my way to the cooking tent to find something to eat and drink. Grabbing a can of peaches, I searched for the can opener. Finding it, I set to work opening my meal. As I squeezed the handle and turned the crank, I broke out in a sweat from pain and effort. By the time I got it opened I was almost too tired to eat and had to force every bite down.

After eating, I went to my tent and lay down, falling asleep instantly.

~ * ~

It was late at night when I woke again. The air was cooler, my head was clearer, and the throb in my shoulder had dulled. Sitting, I decided I should write what happened and what I planned to do in my journal.

Gripping the pen in a shaky hand, I began. . .

~ * ~

Everyone's dead. I killed them all, even my beloved Kate. I don't see why she couldn't have just said thank you and been happy about what I did for us. She broke my heart and stabbed me.

Tomorrow I'll pack up what little food there is and continue north. Harry said that it was safe that way. I'll either find other people or die trying.

I'm proud of myself for saving everyone from the torture of starvation. I should be considered a martyr; I'm living and suffering and they're dead, at peace, free.

Tomorrow I'll set out. Tomorrow I'll live and suffer for humanity.

~ * ~

By the time morning rolled around I'd slept some and packed some. I'd found a bottle of aspirin while I was rummaging through everything and they helped with my pain.

After another quick meal, I started north. I was weak and had to take breaks often. During one break I looked back. Hundreds of birds were circling and feasting on the dead bodies I'd left behind. They looked like a black tornado, swirling down from the sky to wipe away the remnants of death.

Even with my rest stops I made it a good distance the first day and the next. I could feel myself getting weaker after that. On the fourth day I ran out of drinking water.

With no water I gave up hope. I wasn't going to find anyone or anything. I was the last of mankind and I wasn't going to make it. I felt like my body was burning from within as I broke out in a fever, which sapped away even more of my strength.

I trudged onward as long as I could across the never changing dry landscape. Eventually my body gave out and I collapsed. Closing my eyes, I smiled and let myself drift to sleep, hoping I would never wake up.

~ * ~

Slowly I opened my eyes. *Am I dead?* I wondered to myself; I still felt sore and was thirsty. *Do you feel pain and thirst when you're dead?*

I glanced around. My bag was lying beside me. I was naked to the waist except for a bandage around my chest and a sling holding my left arm. I was in a small hut and very much alive. The roof was made up of random pieces of sheet metal; the frame, various pieces of wood and metal shafts; the walls, cardboard and warped plywood.

A panel shifted to my left and a woman ducked inside.

"You're awake," she said with a smile. "We weren't sure if you'd make it. You had a pretty bad infection from the wound on your back."

I grunted and tried to sit up, but fell back, hissing in pain.

"Take it easy," she said, placing a hand on my forehead. "Your fever seems to have broken. Are you hungry?"

"Thirsty," I croaked.

She laughed. "Of course. I'll get you something to drink."

She walked across the room and retrieved a cup of water. She came back and helped me hold my head up while I drank.

"Thank you," I sighed, laying back.

"I'll leave you to rest," she said, heading for the door. "I'll check on you again in a little while."

I nodded and closed my eyes.

I heard the panel shift closed behind her. I couldn't help but think about how much she looked like Kate.

Maybe things will turn out differently this time, I thought as I drifted off to sleep. *Maybe she'll appreciate and love me the way Kate wasn't able to, and we'll have a hope of a future.*

GAME GONE WRONG

Frank Melbourne rushed into his house carrying the box with his new video game system. At thirty-six, he was still a bachelor and didn't have anyone to answer to. He spent his life enjoying whatever caught his attention for the moment. Right now, it was the new game he'd seen on TV. The graphics looked amazing so he'd immediately gone out and bought the game and the system needed to play it.

Still caught up in the adrenaline surge of his purchase, he ripped the system out of its packaging. Once it was free from its cardboard and Styrofoam prison, he began unwrapping the wires and started plugging them in at random, paying no attention to the instructions.

When he was ready to see if everything was working, he stood up and reached for his remote control. His fingers brushed the edge, knocking it off the coffee table. It fell to the floor. He stepped forward to retrieve it and accidentally stepped on it, pushing all the buttons at once. Cursing, he bent down and picked it up. After resetting the TV channel, he pushed more buttons when the system didn't work. Frustrated, he glanced at the instructions, but eventually threw them down with disgust when they didn't tell him exactly what he wanted to know.

Deciding that he should check to make sure the wires were plugged in correctly, he bent over and started wiggling one black cord after another.

Zap!

Frank was thrown violently backwards by electric current.

~ * ~

"Sir, there's been a breach," Lieutenant Armstrong announced, charging up the metal stairs, his military issue black leather boots *thump*ing ominously.

General Beckman glared at the young man like the words coming out of his mouth were toxic waste spewing forth and soiling sacred ground.

"How the hell did that happen?" Beckman barked. "No one knows about this project! There's no way someone could have breached our security web!"

"I don't know, sir," Armstrong said hurriedly. "All I know is a surge bounced off the grid and someone, or something, was transported."

"Find out who and where, or I should say, when," Beckman snapped, turning away. "I want a full report in an hour. National security is at risk and I need answers."

"Yes, sir," Armstrong said, before running back down the stairs and into the bullpen where computer monitors and soldiers were working hard on the new technology they'd invented. They would have to find the breach and the answers needed to fix it before anything else went wrong.

~ * ~

Frank sat up, rubbing the back of his head, which had hit something when he was thrown. He opened his eyes and looked around, wanting to see if anything in his apartment had been damaged. His jaw dropped and he almost stopped breathing from shock.

All around him were tropical trees with vibrant green fronds bigger than his couch. To his right he saw movement, and he quickly turned his head in that direction, wincing at the pain in his head and neck. Absently, he noticed he had a severe burn on his right hand – the one he'd been using to check the wires.

The movement teased his vision again, three feet to the left of the first sighting. Frank struggled to keep up with it, blinking to relieve the blurriness of his eyes.

A tail, he thought, *that's what I saw. A long green and purple tail.*

Something about the glimpse he'd gotten reminded him of a giant lizard.

A long, low, threatening growl emanated from the foliage to his left, not far from his last glimpse of the creature. Quickly and quietly, Frank tried to inch away, looking around frantically for somewhere to hide. He wasn't fast enough.

A monster of a head broke through the greenery and snapped at him with an angry snarl. White pointy teeth, foul breath, and a large orange tongue filled his view.

Frank was paralyzed with fear.

The dinosaur stepped forward, sniffing loudly, before releasing a spine tingling screech. It was over nine feet tall, had long scaly legs that bent backward, and short arms tipped with razor sharp claws. Its coloring was a mixture of glistening purples, yellows, and greens, allowing it to blend with its surroundings unless it wanted to be seen.

Another, similar screech, echoed in the distance. There were more of them and they were coming – Frank could hear them tromping through the jungle in their direction.

He stood and turned to run, coming face to face with another of the creatures. It hissed and snapped at him. Dodging the two reptiles, dancing blindly to the side, he fell over a steep bank that was hidden from him by tall grass. He tumbled head over heels into the river that flowed at the bottom. Sputtering and splashing, he was swept away. He'd managed to escape the creatures, but now he had to battle the current for his life.

It took him a long time to get close enough to the bank for his feet to reach the bottom. By then he was so tired he could barely drag himself from the water. He fell face down on the silty soil of the beach, breathing in painfully large gulps of air. He closed his eyes and flipped over onto his back, looking at the trees and foliage around him. Something in his brain wanted to reject that any of this was real. He tried to tell himself none of it was happening, that dinosaurs were extinct, and he was probably in the hospital on some really good drugs. But the experience of almost drowning, the aching of his muscles, and the vibrance of his surrounds told him it *was* real.

What he wanted to know now was how he'd gotten here, and more importantly, how he was going to get home.

~ * ~

"General Beckman?" Lieutenant Armstrong asked tentatively, entering his superior's office. "I have the report."

Beckman was on the phone, but motioned Armstrong forward into the room. Quickly, he ended the conversation and hung up.

"What have you found?"

Stepping up to the desk, Armstrong handed Beckman an envelope with '**TOP SECRET**' emboldened across it in bright red.

"You'll find all the information we currently have in that file," Armstrong said with confidence.

Beckman laid the file on his desk without opening it. "Why don't you give me the long and short of it? I'll read the technical details later."

Armstrong nodded and linked his hand around his opposite wrist behind his back, and stood with his legs slightly apart. "We now know a man from Kentucky has been transported back in time. We're thinking sometime during the time of Neanderthals, but we aren't exactly sure."

"Shit!" Beckman exclaimed. "How is that possible?"

Armstrong cleared his throat and continued. "Apparently there was an intense power surge and it triggered the hidden technology we've implanted in the new game systems. It was supposed to stay dormant until a certain code was entered. I don't know how he broke it, sir; it was deeply hidden and encrypted."

Beckman sighed and rubbed his forehead. "Remind me why we even put the technology in the games? That doesn't seem like such a bright idea at the moment."

With a stiff nod Armstrong answered, "It was believed once the time traveling operation was off the ground we would need to be able to transport from undisclosed locations around the world. Believing that through the game systems we could spread out our 'locations' to more homes and a wider range of the world, it was implanted, but blocked off so no game 'user' would ever know it was there, or be able to access it."

"Apparently it wasn't hidden well enough."

"It was hidden very well, sir. It shouldn't have happened. We believe the man, Frank Melbourne, might be an operative for another government. I don't know how they found out about what we're doing, but I think there's an inside man – a spy."

Beckman stood and walked to the window of his office that overlooked the bullpen with a heavy sigh. "This is most unfortunate. Do you have any idea who it might be?"

"No, sir. At this time we have no idea, but I do have someone we can trust going through personnel files with a fine tooth comb. I'll let you know if something comes up."

"While you're doing that," Beckman said, "send someone to get Melbourne from the past and bring him back here."

"But, we aren't operational, they might not be able to get ba. . ."

Beckman turned sharply, looking Armstrong in the eye. "I don't want to hear anything about the technology not working. It works. *It has been proven.* Figure it out and get it done. Do I make myself clear?"

"Yes, sir," Armstrong said, saluting and turning to exit the office.

"Oh, and Lieutenant. . ." Beckman said.

Armstrong paused and turned. "Yes, sir?"

"When Frank Melbourne is brought back, you're to be in charge of his interrogation."

The two men's gazes locked and they stared at each other for a moment. Armstrong nodded his understanding. He knew what was expected of him and he had no problem performing his duties. He left the room and closed the door behind him.

Beckman returned to his desk, sat down, and opened the file. He was determined to know everything possible about Melbourne before he arrived.

~ * ~

Frank awoke with a start, surprised he'd fallen asleep. He sat up and looked around. The sun was setting in the distance and the temperature was dropping rapidly, and his clothes were still wet, causing him to shiver.

"I better find somewhere to stay *and* build a fire," he mumbled to himself. He felt lonelier than normal. He did live alone, but if he wanted to see people all he had to do was go somewhere. Here, he was the only one as far as he knew. It hit him that if anything bad happened to him no one would be around to help or save him.

A thought occurred to him. Standing abruptly, he dug in his pocket, withdrawing his cell phone. It was water logged and ruined. He had a feeling that even if it was still functional, he wouldn't have gotten a signal. The conclusion his mind had come to was that he'd somehow been transported back in time, which meant there was no technology.

With a heavy heart and a sense of dread, Frank walked along the river, picking up every piece of dry wood he could find. Even if he didn't have shelter by the time it was dark, he had to have a fire. Otherwise, he would be at the mercy of creatures similar to the ones he'd encountered earlier.

As the world grew darker and darker, Frank decided it was time to make his fire, and perhaps gather some palm fronds to cover himself for the night. It took him mere minutes to build the fire, drawing on his vague memories of being a Boy Scout. He'd been a master at making a fire with a couple of sticks and a string or a shoe lace, and it didn't take him long to feed off of those old skills. He was glad he'd decided to wear his sneakers that day and not his slip-ons, otherwise he would have been in more trouble than he already was.

The fire flared to life just in time. Blackness swallowed the world, and the sounds of predators of the night seeped out of the jungle around him. He sat close to the fire and tried not to be scared. Soon, his exhaustion took over and he fell into a deep sleep.

~ * ~

Armstrong watched as two agents were geared up for time travel. Nothing had been found, yet, in the personnel files or correspondences. Everyone seemed to be clean. He didn't like what was going on. He didn't like that someone had somehow breached their security and he couldn't figure it out.

"We're ready, sir," a lab worker said, sitting at a control panel in front of him.

"Proceed," Armstrong said, hoping the agents wouldn't liquefy and die in the great expanse of time. He turned and left the room after a bright flash of light consumed the agents and they were no more, at least not at the present time.

Walking down the cement walled hallway, stepping in and out of the pools of light cast by the bulbs in the ceiling, he thought about the preparations for his upcoming interrogation. He hadn't used his 'skills' in some time and he was getting excited about flexing his interrogation muscles.

~ * ~

Frank lay shivering in the dark. His fire had gone out and he'd woken from the cold. The sky was filled with clouds, blocking out the light of the moon. With nothing to go by and no way of knowing where he was in this strange place, he crawled around, hoping to find the fire ring he'd made with rocks.

A rumbling growl floated to him on the night's breeze, making him shudder. Holding his breath, he tried to be as quiet as possible while he continued to search for the fireplace, praying there were some coals still burning. If he had to start an entirely new fire it would take time, and he would surely attract whatever was out in the jungle.

When his hand came in contact with ashes, he sighed. They were cold. No coals. No rekindling of the flames would be accomplished.

A twig snapped close-by. Bushes and grass rustled softly, whispering a warning of danger on the move. A roar sounded at the edge of the jungle, and Frank heard something running toward him. He gripped a piece of spare firewood, ready to use it as a club, but he didn't get the chance. Just as he was about to swing at the unknown threat, the hum of a fast flying object whizzed past him and thudded wetly into the creature that was attempting to attack him. It fell to the ground heavily with a groan of defeat. Frank could hear someone behind him, grunting and talking in a language he couldn't understand. Feet padded off the hard packed earth and someone fell on top of him. They both yelped and tried to push the other away.

Someone else called out and the person who'd wrestled with Frank responded, and then all voices went quiet.

Frank heard the people moving around, and then a whisper as someone was sent off. He could hear them moving through the foliage in a rush. Not knowing what to expect, he sat as still as he could, still clutching the branch in case he needed to use it. Light caught his eye off to the right behind him. He turned his head and saw a teenage boy carrying a roughly made, burning torch. The boy was dressed in clothes made from animal skins, but he was clean and he looked fairly intelligent. Once he reached the small clearing where everyone else was waiting, they stared at each other. Standing beside the carcass of a huge feline was a group made up of three men, one woman, and the youth with the torch. They appeared to be as confused as Frank felt.

He slowly got to his feet, still clutching his weapon. He didn't really expect them to be dangerous, but he didn't know. They watched him with blank expressions on their faces, then, all of a sudden, they all started speaking and gesturing at once. He jumped at the noise and movement, watching and listening with fascination. Standing before him were walking, talking cave people.

A blinding flash of bright light blazed from the center of the clearing just as one of the men stepped toward Frank. He closed his eyes and held his arm in front of his face. In that brief moment, before he was completely blinded, he caught a glimpse of two men, dressed in what looked like riot gear on steroids.

Frank lowered his arm and blinked rapidly, trying to see in the semi-darkness. It was even more difficult with the circles of light floating in his vision. He could hear the cave people screaming. A burst from a semi-automatic weapon silenced them. He swallowed, knowing the men had just killed the cave people.

"Who are you?" Frank asked, still blinking and trying to see clearly. He knew it wouldn't do him any good to even try and run away, especially when he couldn't see well and they had guns.

"It doesn't matter who we are. All you need to know is we're here to take you back," one of the men answered briskly.

He didn't respond or move. After what they'd just done, he didn't trust them. But he also didn't want to stay where he was.

The other man, the one who hadn't spoken, approached Frank, and with a well-aimed fist, sent him sprawling, knocking him out.

~ * ~

Armstrong stood silently, watching Frank, wondering what government he worked for, how he'd gotten their technology, and whom he might have told. One thing was definite, he was going to get the name of his contact on the inside if he had to torture him for days.

Slowly, Frank's eyes fluttered open. He moaned, closing them quickly as bright light stabbed through his eyeballs and into his brain.

"Hello?" he croaked. "Is anyone there?"

"How are you feeling, Frank?" Armstrong asked, and moved to stand in front of the light, where he could be seen. The rest of the room was in shadows and hid everyone well. They didn't need to be heard or seen. They just needed information. The information Frank had.

"We want to know who you work for, and who your contact is. If you value your life, you'll tell us now."

"What?" Frank asked, trying to get up, only to realize he was naked and tied to a table that was leaning up at an angle, giving him the illusion of half-standing. "Why am I tied up? Who are you? What's going on?"

"It doesn't matter who I am," Armstrong said. "What matters is who you work for. Tell me!"

The calm, but threatening tone of Armstrong's voice started to scare Frank. He knew the man had to be crazy. He couldn't think of any other reason why the man would be doing this. . .be treating him this way, like he was a criminal.

"I. . .I'm a delivery man. I own my own truck and have contracts with various companies. Why?"

"What do you deliver?"

"Electronics, produce – anything I'm paid to haul," Frank said in a rush, trying to appease the man. "Look, I don't know who you think I am, but this is all a mistake. I just wanted to play a game and somehow ended up on an acid trip in historical hell."

"Who do you make these 'deliveries' to?" Armstrong asked. He knew there was more, he knew Frank was hiding something, and he wanted to know what.

"It varies," Frank stammered. "Last week it was a load of DVD players and game systems to a department store. Why do you care?"

Armstrong looked into the darkness, knowing Beckman was there. Game systems. They needed more information and he knew how to get it, but he had to have permission to do so.

Beckman nodded, and he, and the others, left the room.

Armstrong walked over to a covered tray and pulled back the white towel to reveal an assortment of knives and pliers. Choosing a small, sharp knife, he held it close to Frank's face.

"Tell me who you work for, and I'll make this quick."

Frank was shaking with fear. "I told you who I work for. I deliver stuff! I just wanted to play a game! I don't know what happened! You've got the wrong guy!"

Armstrong smiled and sank the blade into Frank's face until he reached the cheekbone. He paused there, listening to Frank scream and then pant, before his cries of pain subsided into whimpers.

"Who do you work for?" he whispered into Frank's ear.

"I told you, I haul stuff," Frank whined, with tears flowing freely down his face and burning where the small knife had penetrated his skin.

Angling the knife slightly, Armstrong slid it slowly forward toward Frank's nose while holding his head still.

"I can do this all day," he said calmly as Frank convulsed.

Frank shook with gasping spasms, screaming every time he managed to get enough air into his lungs to make even the slightest sound.

Armstrong drew the knife out of Frank's flesh and held it in front of his face. The blood on the cold steel shone a vibrant red in the bright lighting. He could smell the metallic tang of his own blood and feel the throb of his cheek where it'd just been – just blinking caused him excruciating pain.

"I don't know what you want to know," Frank whispered desperately. "If I knew, I would tell you, honest. Please don't continue with this."

With a half-smile smirk, Armstrong looked into Frank's eyes. *He's good,* he thought. *I could almost believe him. He's even managed to bring a sincere light to his eyes, but I'm still not buying it.*

"I don't believe you," Armstrong said, slowly and dramatically transferring the knife to his other hand and pressing the slick blade against Frank's other cheek. "I'll ask you a different question, one you might be more inclined to answer to get the attention off of you. . . Who's your man inside? Who told you about the game and the code?"

Frank frowned, and instantly hissed in pain. "Man inside? Game? Code?"

Armstrong tensed his arm muscles and plunged the blade into Frank's skin, again, to the bone.

Frank cried out and jerked.

"Don't play with me," Armstrong said calmly, watching Frank's eyes, noting pupil size. "Who told you about our operation?"

"I don't know anything about your operation!" Frank screamed before falling into a fit of sobs. "All I wanted to do was play the game. I saw it on TV."

Armstrong, with no expression, cut the side of Frank's face to match the other. He was impervious to his screams. Pain was the vehicle in which he would receive information, and he hadn't even begun to do his worst. He had to admit, he'd expected him to buckle by now. Frank didn't look like the kind of man who would be able to handle such an intense interrogation. He began to wonder which government had trained him. Russia? China? Korea? He didn't look like he had any oriental blood, but then again, agents for hire didn't care who wanted their services as long as they paid well. From the information he'd managed to glean before Frank was brought back, he knew him to be an American citizen all his life, which infuriated him. It was terrible when someone from another country did something like this, but when it was one of your own, one of the people you'd sworn your life to protect, it was a deep betrayal that couldn't be mended.

The torture continued for hours, until Frank finally died from a loss of blood. Armstrong wiped his hands on a towel in disgust, looking down at Frank's mutilated body. He hadn't gotten any of the information he'd been seeking, but he still wasn't convinced of the man's innocence. There was no way he could have hacked into the time travel technology and been transported by accident. Things just didn't happen that way.

Turning away sharply, he marched out of the room and headed for the showers. Blood coated his arms and clothes. He knew after he was cleaned up he would have to tell Beckman he hadn't gotten anything solid. But he vowed to himself that he would find the source, and that he would get the intelligence he needed to protect national security and the project. Whatever it took, he would find the spies who were leaking information and they would pay dearly, just like Frank had.

MYSTERY MEAT

"Brad, there's another bin of meat in the cooler that isn't marked and isn't on the inventory list," Grey Hanson said, stepping into the aisle next to the supervisor as he walked past.

Brad Jenkins stopped suddenly and turned to Grey, looking at him through his clear safety glasses.

"Again?" he asked, taking Grey's clipboard from him and flipping through the pages. "Where is all this meat coming from?"

"I don't know," Grey said. "That's why I wanted to let you know right away. Do you want to come have a look at it?"

Brad nodded and frowned, turning around and heading toward the cooler Grey had just come out of with the middle-aged man following close at his heels.

"It's fresh," Grey said, stepping forward and opening the large silver door for his boss, who was still reading.

"I just wish I knew where it was coming from," Brad said, stepping inside as the cool air created a fog as it rolled out into the large open room. "It's starting to worry me – this is the third time in four months."

Grey followed Brad inside and led him three rows in, to the huge bin of meat that didn't have a tag. Large chunks of red meat with thick layers of fat still clinging to them sat there, waiting to be trimmed and turned into bologna.

Brad handed back the clip board and first inspected the outside of the bin, looking for the date card and the initials of the individual who'd checked it in; he didn't see one. Shaking his head, he pulled a rubber glove out of the right pocket of his white overalls and slid one of his hands inside with the ease of familiarity. He reached forward and squeezed a large chunk of meat, and watched blood run out;

flipping a couple of the others chunks, he repeated the process.

"It's fresh," Brad said, "and is chilled all the way through. It looks to be of fine quality, but the pieces are smaller than I would have expected. Do you think we're getting some left over trimmings from a small, local butcher and it's not included with the main deliveries?"

Grey shrugged. "Could be. But wouldn't there be some record of it somewhere? The office or something? I mean. . .don't we pay them for it?"

"Good point," Brad said, pulling his dirty glove off with a loud snap. "I'll check with the accounting department. Last time I asked at the administration office they looked at me like I'd lost my mind."

"What should we do with it in the meantime?" Grey asked, looking around at the other bins. "It won't stay fresh long and we'll be able to use it today, if you okay it."

"Go ahead," Brad said with a shrug. "There's no sense in letting it go to waste."

"Okay, thanks, Brad," Grey said. "Let me know if you find out something from accounting so I can start logging this stuff properly."

"Will do," Brad said as they both stepped out of the cooler and Grey closed the door. "Have a good day."

They smiled at each other, shook hands, and parted ways, both going about their business and their jobs.

~ * ~

Brad headed upstairs to the supervisors' office area. He was the supervisor for the day shift and had just arrived for the start of shift; Grey had intercepted him on his way in to work. He opened the door to the office he shared with the midnight's supervisor, Hank Renshaw, and was pleased to see he was still there, sitting behind his metal desk, typing information into his computer.

Hank glanced up as the door opened and smiled at Brad, but continued with his work and didn't break his concentration to speak at that exact moment.

Brad sat down and booted his own computer, thinking about what Grey had showed him on the way in. Although it didn't happen often, he was confused and a little disturbed at the mystery meat that kept popping up in the cooler. The bins it showed up in were definitely theirs; they had their brand and name burnt into the sides like all the others.

"Finally!" Hank said, sighing and leaning back in his chair, causing it to squeak loudly while he stretched. "I never thought I would get done with the end of the month report. It's taken me all week to get it typed in. Rene will have to leave me alone for a couple weeks, until I have to do another one." He winked at Brad, and grinned.

Rene Harper was the administrative assistant who did all the 'records' work and made sure they were meeting orders and keeping up production. Her reports went straight to the plant manager. Even though Hank acted like he hated it when she would call and bug him, Brad knew he liked her and was thinking about asking her out now that his divorce was final.

Brad laughed. "Yeah, your phone won't ring at all for the next three weeks! Lucky you."

Hank laughed and sat forward, causing his office chair to squeak again. He turned off his computer and was gathering his stuff while Brad logged into the company's system and checked for any deliveries the previous day and night. There weren't any.

"Hey," Brad said, looking up at Hank who was standing across the room from him, filling his travel coffee cup up for the trip home, "were there any small deliveries last night? Did Norman mention anything, when you came in last night to relieve him, from the afternoon shift?"

Hank frowned and sipped his coffee before he answered. "Nope. Why?"

Brad sighed and picked up a pen from his desk and started tapping it against a small pad of paper in an agitated fashion.

"There's one of those unmarked bins of meat in the main cooler again," he said, dragging his other hand through his short, graying hair.

"Really?" Hank asked. "That's strange. No one has said anything about anything coming in. We had that big shipment a couple days ago from the butchers in Columbus and have been working like mad to get through it while it's fresh. Maybe it came in with those and the sticker fell off or something."

Brad thought for a moment and dropped the pen with a sigh. "Probably, but I still don't like it – this is the third time. You would think they would have learned to be more careful by now if that's what happened."

"You worry too much," Hank said with a laugh. "Just chop it up and use it." He scooped up his belonging and headed for the door, but stopped as he was reaching for the doorknob, turning back. "The owner's son was here for a bit last night, poking around again, so stay on your guard. You don't want to get caught loafing, in case he comes back." He winked, opened the door, and left.

Owen Bradley was set to inherit the Bradley Bologna enterprise once his father passed away, which could be anytime as he was in the hospital and not doing well. The twenty-three-year-old had been visiting the plant more frequently as of late, and there were rumors he was trying to get the place valued so he could sell it once it was his. Everyone was on full alert whenever he was around because they didn't want to be caught loafing or not doing their best with the soon to be new owner on the prowl.

Still slightly upset about the mystery meat – despite Hank telling him not to concern himself – Brad picked up his phone to call accounting to see if he could get some information that would literally take a load off his mind.

~ * ~

Grey's line was working hard that morning and had gotten through four bins in no time – they usually only finished two bins before lunch time. He pulled the unmarked bin up to the line and rolled it up to Delia's table, as she was just finishing up her last one.

"I hope you don't expect me to do all that before lunch," she joked, and winked at him.

Grey laughed. "Nope. But I do expect Jim to help you with it when he's done with what he's trimming." He elbowed Jim, who was standing right behind him, in the back and winked at Delia.

"Sure," Jim said, looking over his shoulder at them, "as long as I don't chop off a finger from being nudged at the wrong moment."

They all laughed and continued to do their jobs, hoping to get their quota in early so they could have an extra-long afternoon break or leave early.

Grey started to take the empty bins to the cleaning station, to keep their work area clear of hazards and paused when he saw Brad coming toward him. The area was down a short corridor, around a corner, and through a doorway covered with heavy, clear plastic strips. He was just getting ready to go through the strips when Brad reached him.

"Hey, Grey," he said, "I got a hold of accounting and they don't have a record of any meat deliveries. I have no idea where that bin came from. Did you get to it yet?"

"Interesting," Grey said. "Yes, I just rolled it up to Delia's station and she started on it. Jim is going to help her when he gets done with the one he's working on. We've done four bins so far this morning! We're on fire." He laughed, but stopped when he noticed Brad didn't look pleased. "What's wrong?"

"I don't know, Grey," Brad said with a sigh. "I just don't get where the meat is coming from, and it worries me. We don't even know what it is!"

Grey nodded. "It's probably coming from one of the big shipments and the tags are falling off or something."

"That's what Hank said before he left," Brad said, and looked around. "I guess I should stop worrying."

"Sounds like a good idea," Grey said, turning back to the bin he was pushing and moved it forward, getting back to work.

"Hey," Brad said, causing him to turn back for a moment. "The prodigal son has been making appearances, so try to keep everyone at least looking busy, okay?"

Grey laughed, nodded, and pushed through the curtain, disappearing.

~ * ~

When Line 3 got back to work after lunch, they were still in high gear and soon had the mystery meat bin emptied. As Delia reached in to retrieve the last chunk of meat, she opened her mouth to holler at Grey to bring them another one, but stopped when she spotted something shiny at the bottom corner of the bin. She frowned and reached in, grabbing a hold of it and bringing it out to wipe it off. She froze and stared at it when she realized what it was – a woman's engagement ring.

Jim turned around to say something to her and paused at the look on her face. He stepped forward and looked at what she was holding in the palm of her hand.

"Where did you get that?" he asked, leaning in closer to get a better look.

"In the bin," Delia said absently, not looking up from the jewelry.

"Someone from one of the butcher shops could have dropped it in. . ." Jim said, reaching up and taking the ring to examine it more closely.

"But, don't they wear gloves?" Delia asked, still skeptical.

"What're you guys doing over there?" Grey yelled in a teasing manner as he came back from taking another bin to the washing station. "Don't you go standing around like that, we have meat to trim."

Delia looked over at him; her face was pale and her eyes were wide inside her safety glasses.

"What's wrong?" he asked anxiously, almost jogging over to where Jim and Delia stood. "What's that?" He reached forward and took the ring from Jim.

"I found that ring in the bottom of this bin," Delia said, nodding at the ring and motioning to the unmarked bin. "Do you think it was. . ." she paused to swallow hard, ". . .contaminated?"

Grey frowned. "I don't know, but we have to assume it was."

He reached over and hit the red emergency stop button on the conveyor belt, stopping the line; the alarms went off and lights started flashing, alerting the supervisor right away that there was an issue. Company policy said that anytime the line was shut down for an emergency, the supervisor of the shift had to restart it. They'd even gone so far in the name of safety as to give the supervisor a special key that unlocked the box with the switch inside to turn off the alarm system so the lines couldn't be started up without it.

While they waited for Brad to make his way to them, the three looked at the bin more carefully and were dismayed and shocked to find a human finger in the sludge at the bottom of the bin as well.

"Oh, God!" Delia exclaimed, gagging and looking away with tears in her eyes.

Jim didn't say anything, but stared at the appendage with an almost solemn express on his face.

Grey, a little freaked out to be holding a severed finger, laid it down on Delia's station table and stepped back as if it would jump up and bite him.

"What's going on?" Brad yelled at the top of his lungs so he could be heard over the alarm. He quickly opened the box with his key and killed the system so they wouldn't have to try to talk over it. "Did someone get hurt?" he asked anxiously.

"Someone. . ." Jim said in a toneless voice.

Brad's head jerked in Jim's direction and a chill ran down his spine as he saw the sad seriousness in the normally jolly man's eyes. The other two employees who worked on the line had gathered around Grey, Delia, and Jim, and were murmuring and staring at the finger and the ring, wondering what misfortune had led to the objects being in the bin.

"Holy shit!" Brad said, finally making his way through the small crowd and noticed what the problem was. "Where did those come from?" He pointed at the ring and finger, and looked around at everyone.

Grey cleared his throat and looked Brad in the eyes. "Delia found the ring in the bin, so I stopped the line. The three of us," he motioned to Jim and Delia, "searched the sludge at the bottom of the bin while we were waiting for you and found the finger."

Delia gagged again when he said 'finger.'

"Where did the bin come from?" Brad asked, turning to the bin and looking for the tag. He glanced up at Grey when he couldn't find one and no one answered his question.

"It's the one I showed you this morning," Grey said quietly.

Brad froze, still half-bent over. "The mystery meat?" he asked in a whisper.

Grey nodded.

With a sigh, Brad stood up and made an announcement to the group.

"I need you all to stay in your overalls and go to the break room," he said. "You'll have to wait there until instructed otherwise by the police."

"What?" Shelly asked, stepping forward. "Why do we have to stay in there when we didn't even work on the bin?" She motioned to herself and Fred, who worked on the other side of the conveyor belt.

Brad looked her in the eyes. "I don't know what the police will want to check out when they get here. If they say you're clear, then you can go and shower, but until then, you have to stay put."

Shelly opened her mouth to protest again, but Grey ushered them all toward the break room and away from the 'remains' of someone.

~ * ~

It was seven o'clock at night and Brad was still in the factory, alone. He was in full gear, hosing down the line, the tables, and the floors, and getting ready to scrub them down. He knew it would take him hours to do what the people who worked on the line would have done together in less than forty-five minutes, and he wasn't looking forward to it.

He'd canceled the afternoon shift, as the police had instructed him to, so they could investigate the bin and, possibly, its origins. The day shift had been sent home at four o'clock when their shift had ended, leaving him to deal with the officers and forensics team, and after they left, the mess of Line 3. The forensics team had taken all the bologna that had come from Line 3 that day, in case it bore any evidence. He didn't argue with them when they'd asked for it, since he'd known they would have to scrap it all anyway.

After an hour and a half of hosing and scrubbing, he'd finished one side of the line and decided it was time to take a break. Stretching his aching back, he headed for the break room, eager to sit down and give his lower back a rest. He'd no more than sat down when a loud bump sounded beyond one of the windows that looked out on the plant, close-by one of the doors leading to outside. He listened for a few minutes, and not hearing anything else, he went back to relaxing. Kicking his feet up onto a chair, he leaned his head back against the break room wall, letting the events of the day roll through his mind; everything was a jumble and he was fighting hard to make sense of it all.

A jingle and another loud bumping noise – sounding like something slamming into a doorjamb as it was forced through a tight doorway – echoed through the silent plant from the same door he'd thought he'd heard something coming through before.

He stood slowly and walked over to the window between the break room and the plant floor, wondering if maybe Norman had come in to help him or to make sure things were all right. He was shocked to see Owen Bradley lugging a heavy box through the door and into the factory.

He turned and headed for the doorway, hoping to intercept Owen and see what was going on, but he'd vanished by the time he'd left the break room and circled around to the door where he'd entered the facility. Frowning, Brad scanned the area, wondering where he could have gone.

Thinking maybe he'd headed up to the offices, Brad headed that way, but stopped in mid stride when he heard a commotion from the cooler area. He changed direction and walked toward the cooler quietly. He arrived to see the door standing wide open; the fog obscured his view of the inside of the cooler, but he could vaguely make out a human form within, moving things around. He proceeded closer to get a better view.

Owen was inside the cooler, transferring meat from a plastic lined cardboard box, into one of the rolling bins they stored meat in.

"What the hell are you doing?" Brad asked, rushing into the cooler without thinking about it.

Owen froze and spun around in surprise. "Oh, Brad!" he exclaimed, clutching his chest. "You scared me! What are you doing here? I thought the plant was shut down for the night."

"I stayed to clean up," Brad said, and then returned to his ranting. "What the hell are you doing? You can't just go adding meat in without going through the proper channels! That's how we wound up with the problem we had earlier!" As he yelled at Owen, something clicked in his mind and everything that had been bugging him fell into place. "It was you. . ." he said in an almost whisper. "You're the one who has been putting the meat in the unmarked bins. But. . .the ring and finger. . ."

Brad stopped, noticing that Owen was wearing a broad grin on his smug face.

"Yeah, that was Beth," he said snidely. "She was a cheating whore, so I decided not to marry her. She was pregnant though, and I'll be damned if I'll pay for a kid that's not mine." He paused and shrugged. "Had to get rid of the body somehow, and what better way to do it than here." He waved his arm over the bins of meat. "I had most of her in that bin, but there were still some little pieces I didn't get to chop up."

Brad fought the nausea that made his stomach roll. "What about the other bins? There were three. . ." he said while trying to back out of the cooler so he could shut Owen inside and call the police. "That's a lot of meat for one woman."

Owen laughed. "Oh, those were the men she was fucking. I made them disappear one at a time. It was almost priceless to see the expression on her face every time one of them vanished. She didn't think I knew, but damn was she stupid."

"This is wrong, Owen," Brad said, still inching his way backward, "you can't just chop people up and feed them to other people, and besides, if they were sleeping around, they could have had diseases."

"You know," Owen said, dumping the rest of the contents of the box into a bin, "I really hadn't thought about that. I don't eat bologna, so I don't care anyhow." He shrugged and focused on Brad as he pulled a small pistol from the waistband of his designer pants. "Where do you think you're going, anyway? Going to call the police and tell on me? Well. . .I can't allow that to happen, now can I?"

Brad raised his hands in supplication. "It doesn't have to go down like this, Owen. I'll make a deal with you. . .I won't tell if you don't do this anymore. Okay?"

"Good try," Owen said, laughing. "Not gonna work though. I know your type – always having to do the right thing. I've been watching you and the other supervisors, and you're the one who does everything by the book. No, you have to die."

Without warning, Owen pulled the trigger three times and the *boom*s from the pistol echoed loudly off the cooler walls.

A look of shocked pain danced across Brad's face, before it went slack and he fell to the floor with a dull *thud*, dead.

Owen walked over to the corpse of the fallen supervisor and sighed. "Now I have more work to do tonight. You've spoiled my plans." He tucked the gun back into his waistband and grabbed a hold of Brad's ankle, dragging him out of the cooler. "It's okay though, I'll take out my frustration chopping you up!"

~ * ~

One week later. . .

"Has anyone heard from Brad?" Grey asked as they suited up for work.

"No," Fred said with a sad sigh.

Jim shook his head and continued putting on his overalls.

Grey sighed. "I still can't believe he killed all those people and chopped them up. It just doesn't mesh with how he acted. Do you think they'll ever catch him and find out for sure if he's the one who did it?"

Fred shrugged. "Don't know."

"Hey," Hank yelled as he poked his head in through the door, "hurry up, Owen's here to make some kind of announcement. I think owning the plant has gone to his head. . ." He laughed half-heartedly and disappeared from view.

The three men looked at each other, knowing Hank was having a hard go of things. Not only was Brad missing, but he and Norman were picking up the slack until someone replaced him. He also wasn't happy because Rene was dating Owen. Everyone knew he liked her, and they all felt a bit sorry for him.

Ten minutes later, all the employees of the day shift were in a semicircle around the platform in front of the supervisors' office. Owen stood above them – with Rene a step behind him, beaming happily – and started his speech, saying he was going to keep everything running like it had been since the beginning of Bradley's Bologna, and how everyone would still have a job, blah, blah, blah.

Grey blocked out the spiel; he'd heard it all before. Every time management or ownership changed hands, it was the same old shit. Lies, upon lies of how nothing would change, when they knew everything would. It wasn't until Owen pulled Rene forward and announced their engagement that he refocused on what was going on. He looked up to see her beaming from ear to ear, holding up her hand to show off the engagement ring.

Half-hearted congratulations and cheers echoed through the plant, but Grey didn't join in. Something about the style of the ring looked familiar, and with a startled gasp, he realized that it was almost exactly the same to the one they'd found in the mystery meat bin. His mind was a jumble of questions and he made a decision right then. He would get Owen alone and he would ask him some straightforward questions. His opportunity came later that day, at the end of shift. He stayed a few extra moments and corned Owen in the administration office. They were alone, as everyone else had left for the day and the afternoon shift would be coming in soon.

Grey asked some questions, Owen introduced him to his gun, and there was an extra meat bin in the cooler once again.

~ * ~

The next morning, Hank came out to Line 3 and looked around.

"Has anyone heard from Grey?" he asked. "He didn't call off this morning, but he's not here, which is highly unlike him."

Everyone frowned and shook their heads no.

Hank sighed. "Okay, go ahead and get to work. You'll have to pull your own bins today though, because I don't have anyone to replace him."

They all mumbled and murmured as they headed to the cooler.

Shelly didn't notice that her bin didn't have a tag, since they weren't used to pulling bins from the cooler, so she didn't know that she was trimming and feeding Grey's remains to the conveyer belt, or to the masses as the bologna went out the door a few days later.

The consumers had no idea what was in the packages of Bradley's Bologna when they opened them. Who knew what was really in bologna anyway? Wasn't it just a strange form of mystery meat to eat on a sandwich?

FATHER'S REVENGE

I still remember the first time I saw you.

You were walking toward to barn with my father, talking.

My mother told me that you knew about the horses my father wanted to breed, and that he'd hired you to help.

My young heart fluttered at the sight of you, although that day I didn't even see your face. I knew there was something different about you, something special. I knew I wouldn't stop until I found out what it was, and since you were staying, I didn't have to hurry.

I pretended I was interested in the horses so that I would have a reason to visit the barn, to be near you, to learn about you.

I'll never forget the first riding lesson you gave me, when you put your hand on my thigh and made sure I was steady. Or the way you looked up at me and smiled encouragingly, your hazel eyes twinkling in the sun.

At that moment I knew that I loved you. I didn't care that you were thirty-five and I was eighteen. Age didn't matter, only the feelings I had for you did. They felt so right, so special.

I agonized for months about whether I should tell you or not. You didn't seem to have an interest in me. I was young and shy and didn't know how to make my attraction to you known.

I had dreams about you almost every night, dreams so intense that when I awoke, I wanted to run to your apartment behind the barn and beg you to make me yours. But, I was afraid. Afraid of the strength of my feelings, of what my parents might do if they found out, of you rejecting me.

Eventually I couldn't hold myself back any longer. I had to do something. I decided on the day and time that I would come to you. I planned what I would wear, what I would say. I was ready to give myself to you, and I hoped that you would take my gift, my love for you.

I snuck out after dark – hours after everyone had gone to bed. Making my way through the red and black barn behind our house, I saw that your light was still on.

My heart jumped into my throat and I stared. I was excited that you were still awake, yet scared that I was making a mistake.

I steeled my will, and putting one foot in front of the other, found my way to your door. I lifted my hand and was about to knock when I heard moaning and panting float out of the open window.

Frowning, I peeked inside.

You were awake, but you weren't alone. My mother was with you. Both of you were naked, and you were doing the things that I'd dreamed about, but not with me, with her.

I turned away, pressing my back against the side of the guest house, scared I would be noticed. Hot tears slid down my cheeks and dripped onto the pink cotton dress that I'd worn just for you.

Gasping for breath, my heart burning with pain, I ran back to the house. I no longer cared if I was heard as I slammed the door behind me. I ran up the stairs, and into my room, slamming yet another door.

I woke my father.

Soon there was a knocking on my door.

I didn't answer.

My father came in and asked me what was wrong.

I wouldn't tell him.

He persisted and asked me where my mother was, if she was hurt.

I shook my head, pressing my face into my pillow so he wouldn't see the hurt in my eyes.

He rubbed my back until I fell asleep, not pushing me to confide in him.

The next morning, I awoke fully dressed, my eyes hot and red from crying. I didn't want to get out of bed. I didn't care about life or anything to do with it.

Nothing mattered. You had betrayed my heart.

Eventually I went downstairs, dreading coming face to face with my mother.

I turned into the kitchen and froze in shock. Blood covered the white tiles of the kitchen floor. There were hand prints in it, like someone had tried to get a grip on the slippery surface as they were dragged out the back door.

I carefully stepped around as much of the bright red liquid as I could, and made my way outside.

I saw something hanging from the rafters of the barn. A voice in my head told me to turn around, go back upstairs, and pretend I hadn't seen anything. But, another voice urged me on to discover what had happened. I should've listened to the first voice, but I didn't.

I went to investigate.

I walked slowly through the yard, each step taking me closer to the barn. I could hear the horses whinnying and shifting nervously as I got closer. But, it wasn't me that had them stirred up.

I was close enough now to see that the hanging objects were you and my mother. You both were hung by nooses. Your bodies were cut and bleeding.

You were both dead.

I screamed and screamed. The horses joined me in horror, their whinnies intensifying.

I turned to leave, to run back to the house and get help.

I collided with my father's chest.

He was covered in blood. He looked down at me with vacant eyes.

I knew that he'd done it. He'd killed you and mother.

He must have found you after I'd gone to sleep, and exacted revenge.

Father went to jail, but I'm still free.

I remember you every time I see a barn. I remember my love and my pain. I remember Father's revenge.

INNOCENT BLOOD

Rachel sat in the car, watching her husband in the café, having lunch with a woman she'd never seen before. For weeks she'd suspected he was keeping secrets from her. Now she knew the truth. He was cheating on her; the evidence was right before her eyes.

She watched them talk and laugh with her heart aching in her chest, as she wondered: *What have I done to cause him to seek out another woman? Why aren't I good enough?*

As she sat there watching them her hurt turned into anger. She decided she would show him she was a force to be reckoned with.

Starting the engine with a violent twist of the key in the ignition, she sped away with an idea forming in her head. She had just hours to get things ready. He would have the surprise of his life waiting when he got home from work.

~ * ~

Rachel pulled into the garage and waited for the door to close behind her before getting out. She had a lot to do and time was growing short. She also didn't want some nosy neighbor ruining things before they began.

Getting out, she started to unload everything she'd bought. She was especially careful with the white plastic container of leeches and the small aquarium of electric eels in the trunk, which she'd purchased at a local specialty fish store. She'd worked there part time a few months ago and had learned a lot about aquatic life.

Living by the ocean defiantly had its perks. You could find almost anything at the local markets – things that had been caught and others that were used for bait. That was how she'd found two good sized live lobsters. The boat had just been docking when she'd finished loading the eels.

After those were safely inside, she went back out and extracted the largest of her purchases from the back seat – the stuffed and mounted sword fish. It was wrapped in brown paper and was very heavy.

Once she had everything inside, she stood for a moment grinning. If anyone had been there to see her, they would have noticed the demented look in her eyes.

~ * ~

Jason came home right on time.

"Honey, I'm home," he called as he came in from the garage. "I smell fish. Are we having fish for supper?"

Dropping his keys on the counter, he frowned. Nothing was cooking. Usually Rachel had something started when he got home from work.

"Honey?" he called, heading toward the hall.

He stopped dead in his tracks as he finally spotted his wife. She was standing in the archway that led to their bedroom, wearing a red velvet teddy and nothing else.

"I've been waiting for you," she purred, and walked slowly forward. She wrapped her arms around his neck and kissed him.

He grinned and kissed her back.

She pulled back, bit her bottom lip, and pulled him by his hand into the bedroom. There were candles sitting on every available surface, casting a warm, seductive glow across the bed.

"This is a nice surprise," he said, pulling her to him and kissing her again.

She pulled away and shook her head when he tried to lay her back on the bed. "I have plans for you."

He laughed. "Okay, I'm all yours."

"Take off your shirt and lay on the bed," she said.

Grinning, he did as he was told.

Rachel climbed up on the bed and straddled him. Taking his wrists, she pulled them above his head and tied them to the headboard with silk scarves.

"Feeling frisky, are you?" Jason asked, getting a great view down the bodice of her teddy as she leaned over him.

"Something like that," she said, grinding on him before climbed off.

"Where are you going?"

"Not far," she said, picking up the remote and turning on a video she had ready in the TV. "I thought you might like some extra stimulation."

A tingle of excitement went through Jason as he watched the naked people on the TV. His wife had never shown signs of being *this* kinky before.

Maybe she got some ideas from one of those women's magazines that she always reads, he thought fleetingly.

Mentally shrugging, he decided he might as well enjoy it.

Rachel got back on the bed and, being careful not to block his view of the TV, she skimmed her fingers down over his chest until she reached his belt. She unbuckled it slowly. She grinned in satisfaction when he groaned and closed his eyes briefly. Unzipping his pants, she giggled as he raised his hips, trying to get her to touch him.

Before long she had him stripped naked. That's when she pulled out the little white plastic container.

"What's that?" Jason asked.

"A surprise for you," she said with a laugh.

Something about the sound seemed off to him, it held a touch of harsh, and a lot of crazy. Warning bells went off in his head. He tugged at his wrists, trying to free them, but they were tied tight.

"Rachel, untie me," he insisted.

"Hmm, I don't think so," she said, smiling and opening the container. "We've just begun our fun for the night."

Getting up on the bed, she straddled his legs, sitting back on them with all of her weight. Extracting a black worm from the container, she quickly laid it across his erection.

"What the hell is that?" he asked, trying to buck and wiggle his hips to throw it off.

"It's a leech," she said calmly, adding another.

"Get them off me!"

"Darling, I thought you liked to be sucked. Doesn't your girlfriend suck it for you? Might as well let them suck it too, since you like to share."

"Who? I don't have a girlfriend! What the fuck is wrong with you, woman?" he screamed. "Get those damn things off of me!"

"What's wrong with me?" she screamed back. "Who was that woman you were having lunch with? You've been cheating on me and now you are going to get what you deserve!"

Hurriedly, she added the rest of the dozen leeches.

"She's just a friend. I haven't been cheating on you," Jason screamed, still trying to shake the leeches off. "I would never cheat on you! I love you. Please take these things off."

Rachel laughed and got up off the bed. "I don't believe you. I saw you with her. I saw how she tossed her hair, how she looked at you. I saw the way you looked at her, how you touched her hand. Nothing you say can change my mind. You can't convince me that what I saw with my own eyes isn't the truth."

"You're crazy," he screamed. "She's . . ."

She picked up the remote and turned the TV up full volume, drowning him out.

He thrashed and kicked as she pulled a heavy pair of rubber gloves out from under the bed and put them on.

She calmly walked over to the closet and pulled out the pair of lobsters. Bringing them back over, she took the rubber bands off of their claws and lay them on his chest. They started pinching him, cutting his skin, and pulling off chunks of flesh.

Jason screamed as one of them pinched and tore off his nipple.

Rachel just stood beside the bed watching with a demented, gleeful look in her eyes as he suffered. The sounds of moaning and flesh meeting in sensual pleasure on the video covered everything else. She started getting excited as his blood flowed from the wounds. She'd never realized torture could be so arousing.

When the lobsters started to wander off, she picked them back up and laid them on his chest again. They kept pinching and pulling, and he kept screaming.

After a while, she decided the lobsters weren't enough fun anymore, and started to pick off the leeches, dropping them back into their container. She enjoyed the look of fear in his eyes as he watched her, waiting to see what they had done to his dick. The spots where they had been connected were bleeding, and there had been enough of them that his genitals were covered in blood. It flowed freely at first, because of the leech's saliva that caused the blood not to clot. But, after a few moments, the bleeding started to slow.

Jason wasn't paying attention to Rachel. He was too busy worrying about the damage. So when she reappeared beside the bed holding a dripping, hissing electric eel, he jumped.

Shaking his head, he tried to kick her away. But he missed her and kicked the eel's tail instead. The numbing buzz of its electric charge stunned him, causing that leg to become useless. He continued to kick at her with the other, and she simply touched the eel's tail to it as well, rendering them both immobile long enough for her to put the eel back into the small aquarium and get another.

She had a hard time carrying the second one, it was wriggling and the rubber gloves didn't have any grips on them. But she finally got the wet creature under control and brought it to the bed.

Jason could feel the cold water dripping on his skin as she bent over and quickly wrapped the eel's tail around his genitals. His whole body jerked as electricity course through his blood stream. It didn't last long, but it was enough to stun his entire body.

Rachel put the eel back in the aquarium with the others and then turned off the TV. The room was completely silent as she sat on the edge of the bed and looked at her husband. His eyes were vacant as they stared off into space. She feared the eel might have killed him, and that she wouldn't get to have any more fun, but he was still breathing.

Lovingly she stroked one of the lobsters as she put it down between his legs, hoping it would grab onto something sensitive.

Something inside broke loose as she sat there and she started screaming at him. She loved him so much. She just couldn't understand why he'd cheated on her. She didn't know what she wasn't giving him that some other woman was able to.

All the hurt and anguish came pouring out of her, and before she knew it she was pounding on his chest, yelling incoherent things at him. Begging him to love her and then yelling at him for hurting her.

By the time she calmed down, he was starting to stir. She decided it was time to finish this, now tired of the whole thing.

She trudging over to the closet – the adrenaline rush her anger had given her was now gone. She was drained from her emotional outburst and no longer felt anything. It was all mechanics – what was planned and had to be done. She just wanted to get it over with.

Kneeling down, she unwrapped the small sword fish she'd bought. It was stuffed and mounted. She hadn't been able to find a live one. Besides a live one would have been too heavy for her to lift and use for what she had planned.

Walking over to the bed, she raised it up and forcibly slammed the sword beak of its upper jaw into his chest twice, puncturing one lung and then the other.

Standing beside the bed, holding the board with the mounted fish, she watched her husband struggle for breath. Pink bubbles rose from the holes in his chest and his mouth.

She jumped when the phone rang.

With a sigh, she answered it. "Hello?"

"Hi," a feminine voice replied. "Is Jason there?"

Anger surged from the depths of Rachel's soul knowing this had to be the woman.

"No," Rachel snapped. "He's not. Would you like to leave a message?"

The woman was silent for a long moment. "Well, I guess I could talk to you. Or is this a bad time?"

"You can talk to me," Rachel said flatly, as she watched Jason take his last breath.

"I don't know if he did yet, but Jason was supposed to tell you about me," the woman said. "I'm Joyce, a friend of his from college."

"Oh, really?" Rachel asked.

"We lost touch and I found him on a social media site a couple weeks ago. Since then we've been talking and meeting for lunch every once in a while."

"Oh," Rachel said. "Why didn't he tell me?"

"He wanted to, but I asked him not to. I've been having some personal issues from a bad break up. I had a stalker and I didn't want to bring anyone else into it. Everything was cleared up today and he was going to tell you about me when he got home. He said something about meeting for dinner or something sometime. My girlfriend was all for it."

Rachel couldn't breathe. All she could hear was the thump of her heart as her blood pumped through her body. Jason hadn't cheated on her. The woman was a lesbian! She'd just tortured and killed her husband and he had never done anything to deserve it.

She told Joyce she would give Jason the message and quickly got off the phone. Instantly, she started to cry. Guilt and loss weighed heavily on her. She couldn't undo what she'd done. She didn't know what she was going to do now.

She started to panic, looking down at her husband's dead body. She had to get him out of there. His very presence was making her uneasy. Quickly, she put the lobsters away and got dressed.

She wrapped his body in plastic and dragged him out to the SUV. Luckily for her, the plastic made it easier to move the body, at least until she got to the garage. But, since it had gone so well on the carpeting in the house, she grabbed the welcome mats she had in front of the door and laid them in a path to the hatchback. After that, it was a bit easier.

Once she got back there, she put his legs up in the cargo area, but wasn't able to lift his torso at the same time; he was too heavy and bulky.

Panting and sweating, she leaned her hip against the bumper and tried to calm down and think rationally. While she was looking around, she noticed a length of yellow nylon rope hanging on the wall. It gave her an idea.

Grabbing it off the peg, she quickly uncoiled it and tied an end around Jason's ankles, then climbed into the cargo area of the SUV. She crawled over the back seat and out through the left passenger's door, still holding the other end of the rope. Wrapping it around her arm, she put all of her weight into pulling him up and into the SUV. Once she had most of his body loaded, she tied her end of the rope to the handle of the door that led into the house.

Rushing around the back of the vehicle, she pushed him the rest of the way in and after untying the rope, she coiled the slack and put it on the backseat. She went back in and got the eels, lobsters, and leeches, putting them in the back with Jason. After closing the hatch and making sure it was secure, Rachel got in and hit the button to open the garage door.

The darkness of night was welcome. She hadn't realized how much time had passed since Jason had come home, and she'd started torturing him. As she drove to the pier to dump the body, she cried and lamented what she'd done. She was so upset that she almost drove off the road a couple of times. Luckily there was no one around to notice.

She was happy to see the pier was deserted. It was probably because of the overcast sky. No one wanted to be around the water when it was about to storm.

As fast as she could, Rachel dumped Jason's body and the water creatures into the ocean. She was hoping that with the wind kicking up they would be washed out to sea and no one would ever know what had happened. She planned to file a missing person's report in a couple of days, figuring that would be enough time before saying anything was wrong.

It only took her fifteen minutes to dump everything, but it seemed like an eternity to her. She kept glancing over her shoulder, expecting someone to be standing right there and catch her red handed. No one did.

No sooner had she gotten back into the SUV than the sky let loose a torrent of fat rain drops. They made driving home difficult. Between the blurred windshield and her blurred vision from tears, she could only drive thirty-five miles per hour.

Once she arrived home, she took the rope, the blanket off the bed, the sword fish, and the clothes she was wearing and burned them in the living room fire place. As flames consumed them, she thought about her life and how the heat of jealousy had destroyed everything. Lying down on the couch, she watched the fire consume the evidence until she fell asleep.

~ * ~

A couple of days later, Rachel called the police and reported Jason missing. She'd decided to say that he'd come home from work, and then decided to go for a walk to the pier. It was something he frequently did, so it wouldn't raise suspicion with the neighbors if they were questioned.

Joyce kept calling. After she'd made the report, Rachel told her that he'd gone missing. She was upset and said to let her know as soon as Rachel heard anything.

~ * ~

A full month after filing the missing person's report, the police showed up on Rachel's doorstep.

"Yes," Rachel said, answering the door. "Have you found anything out? Have you found my husband?"

She was thinking she should get an acting award for what a good job she was doing when the tall, balding officer took off his hat and shuffled his feet.

"We've found his body, ma'am," he said nervously, glancing at his partner. "He washed up on shore and was discovered yesterday morning."

Rachel gasped and covered her mouth with her hand. "His body?"

The other officer stepped forward. "'Fraid so, ma'am. Looks like he'd been in the water a while. Fish bites all over him. He's at the morgue now, we'll need you to stop by and identify the body. If you'd like, we can take you and bring you home. I don't think it would be wise for you to drive right now."

Rachel nodded, tears sliding down her cheeks. She knew the officers thought it was because she was in shock and upset because she'd just found out her husband was dead. She knew it was from guilt, remorse, and loss.

She went with the officers and did what she needed to do. She signed a paper for them to do an autopsy, and went home. She didn't sleep that night, too worried they would find something that would trace it all back to her.

It was days before she heard anything more.

The autopsy reported that there was no water in his lungs and there was bruising on his wrists. They suspected foul play, but they had no more evidence to go on. It was ruled a homicide. There were no leads.

~ * ~

That was when the weird things started happening. Rachel would come home and there would be wet footprints on the floor leading to the bedroom, and the bed would be soaked.

One morning there was a pair of lobsters crawling around on the kitchen floor. They were still wet, like they had just been taken out of a tank.

Leeches had filled the sink in the bathroom while she'd been out for the day.

Each time, she'd gotten rid of the evidence, not saying a word to anyone. She knew Jason was haunting her, so she put the house up for sale. In days she had an offer.

~ * ~

Rachel came home from signing the papers at the realtor's. The house was sold. She had sixty days to move out, which was fine with her; she already had half of her stuff packed.

With a sigh of relief, knowing she would be far away soon and the haunting would end for her, she went to take a hot shower.

She turned on the shower and took off her clothes. Without looking, she stepped into the tub. A sudden jolt of electricity coursed through her body. In a moment her eyes took in the bathtub half-full of water, swarming with electric eels. With all of them combined, she went completely numb in an instant. Paralyzed she fell and hit her head on the toilet. With all her weight behind the blow, the porcelain caved in her skull and ended her life.

~ * ~

When her body was found, the eels were gone and the shower was still running. Her death was declared an unfortunate accident. But, it wasn't. It was the revenge of a ghost...innocent blood that had to have retribution.

ON ACCOUNT OF BACON

"Now tell me everything leading up to the events that got you arrested."

I looked at the pompous attorney. I knew he wouldn't believe me if I told him. Silently I sat there, twisting my wrists back and forth inside the cold steel circles of my handcuffs, staring straight ahead.

Sighing, the attorney looked up at me over the rims of his too-large glasses.

"I can't help you if you don't tell me what happened," he said.

I looked down at my lap, at my hands clasped together – knuckles white and jutting. I could feel my jaw muscles tightening, clamping my teeth together. I reared back, causing my chains to clang against the table and the legs of my chair. I looked this idiot-man-in-a-suit in the eye.

"You won't believe me! Why should I tell you anything?"

He blinked at me for a moment, withdrawing his hands from the small metal table between us.

"I'll believe you," he said, but his eyes said he was lying.

Biting my bottom lip, I thought for a moment; it might be worth telling this smug idiot the whole story, just to see his reaction.

"Leslie?"

"Okay. . ." I sighed. "I'll tell you everything, but you have to promise to sit there and not say a damn word until I'm done."

Sitting forward, I leaned my arms on the table.

"Deal?" I asked.

The attorney nodded.

I could see he was confused by my abrupt mood change, but I didn't really care. Let him wonder.

"Well, it all started when I was seventeen. My dad died, and my mom lost her job when the factory closed. She couldn't afford to take care of me, so I was sent to live with my mom's sister and her husband. My aunt and uncle lived on a farm; they raised chickens, cows, and pigs."

The attorney raised his eyebrows and opened his mouth to speak.

I held up my hands and shook my head.

"You promised," I said.

He nodded and shut his gaping hole.

"Anyway," I continued. "I was sent to live at their farm. At first it wasn't too bad: Aunt Tisha was really nice and caring; and her husband was always busy with the animals. Their lives ran like clockwork – getting up, making breakfast, taking care of the animals, all the normal farming stuff.

"When I first arrived, school was still in, so I was away from the house for the most part. I remember being eager for that summer to start – I had plans of getting a job at the local diner waiting tables and having some spending money. I'd made lots of friends at school; country people are actually as friendly as I'd heard they were."

I smiled, thinking about the warm welcome I'd received at Riverside High.

"It seems so childish now, how eager I was to have a summer of fun and freedom before my senior year of high school. I was even thinking about what college I might want to go to – someplace fun, but that could also build me a good future through a decent education."

Sighing, I lifted my hands to tuck my curly blonde hair behind my ear. The handcuffs were a pain, because I had to remember to use both hands all the time instead of just one.

"I was out of school for a week, working at my new job. Life was great. My mom had even found a job, so I was supposed to move back home in a couple of months. I was actually happy for the first time since before my dad died. Then it happened. I woke up early on a Saturday and heard my uncle yelling at my aunt."

I paused and took a deep breath.

"He was yelling at her because she'd burnt the bacon. That's like sacrilege to Uncle Troy. If you burn the bacon, it's as bad as wrecking his truck or a tornado destroying the house. He was flipping out on her. I'd never heard him yell like that before.

"I heard a smacking sound, my aunt scream, and then a thump. I raced down the stairs to see what was going on. I was scared, but I wanted to make sure my aunt was all right. I would have never gone down there if I'd known what was going to happen."

I reached for the paper cup filled with water that had been placed on the table for me. I picked it up with a trembling hand and took a few slow sips. Setting it back down, I reminded myself to breathe.

"It was horrible. Uncle Troy was standing over Aunt Tisha. She lay flat on her back on the floor in front of the stove. He raised his fist to strike her again, and she was crying and trying to wiggle away.

"Aunt Tisha was a big woman, easily three hundred pounds; she couldn't move very fast. He hit her hard in the face. Then he hit her again as I ran through the kitchen, yelling for him to stop. With the second blow he'd knocked her out.

"I grabbed his arm, still screaming. He pushed me away and kicked my aunt in the stomach, although she was already unconscious. I grabbed his arm again. This time he grabbed me by the hair and threw me into one of the hardwood kitchen chairs; it fell backward and my head hit the floor. The blow stunned me, but I vaguely remember him correcting the chair and tying me to it. He tied my legs to the two front legs of the chair, looped the rope around my neck and then tied my wrists to the back legs. He had the rope run in a way that made it tighten around my neck if I moved my wrists or legs. I had to sit with my back arched, just to keep from strangling myself. He stepped into the laundry room and came back with one of his bandanas; he rolled it up and used it to gag me.

"After he finished tying me, he went over and drug Aunt Tisha off the floor and put her in a chair as well. He was extremely strong from doing the farm work and moved her like she was nothing more than a limp rag doll. She started coming to while he was moving her, which seemed to please him.

"He used a roll of duct tape to imprison her in another of the kitchen chairs, growling and swearing at her. All I could get out of it was 'bacon' every few words – mostly because he would scream the word at her.

"The kitchen was filling with smoke from the bacon that was still on the stove, burning. Uncle Troy seemed to get more and more agitated. He started rooting through drawers, until he found a silicone brush that Aunt Tisha used when she needed to baste something.

"The look in his eyes was psychotic. With a huge grin on his face, he dipped the brush into the bacon grease sizzling in the skillet. He turned toward Aunt Tisha and touched it to the tip of her nose. She screamed, shaking her head like a dog trying to get a certain taste out of its mouth.

"Uncle Troy laughed; it was the most evil laugh I'd ever heard, causing goose bumps to break out on my arms and legs.

"He dipped the brush in the bacon grease again, grabbed Aunt Tisha's hair and held her head still. He brushed the hot bacon grease down across both her cheek bones, like he was putting blush on her backwards.

"She was no longer screaming, she was shrieking like a crazy person. Her whole body was shaking with the effort to free herself from her bonds. I could smell her flesh burning – the scent mixed with the aroma of bacon. Every breath I pulled into my lungs made me gag.

"I knew Uncle Troy wasn't worried about anyone hearing the shrieks and screams Aunt Tisha was bellowing – living on a 300-acre farm, he knew no one would hear us, and no one would come to our rescue.

"Aunt Tisha was begging him to stop, pleading between each massive sob that racked her body. What he did to her was terrible. He just kept dipping and painting, until all the skin of her face was fried. But the worst of it all was when he held her eyelids open and let bacon grease drip into her eyes. I looked away and wished I could disappear. The sounds she made were almost not human. I couldn't even imagine the pain she was suffering. I felt bad for her, but at the same time, I was praying I wasn't next.

"I thought the bacon grease in the eye thing was the worst he was going to do to her, but I was wrong. He picked up the entire skillet of hot bacon grease and held her head while he dumped it down her throat, telling her that she could eat the crap she'd made. His body blocked my view of his actions, but I knew what he was doing, and I knew there was nothing I could do to stop him. I couldn't even move without choking myself. I realized I was crying, that my tank top was soaked with tears, and that I was trembling.

"Aunt Tisha's body lurched violently. I heard strangling noises, saw one more violent attempt of her body to fight off the onslaught, and then she was still – too still. Uncle Troy placed the skillet in the sink with a smile on his face and pleasure in his eyes."

I stopped talking and looked at the attorney. His expression was one of total disgust and blatant disbelief. I'd seen it happen and it was still hard for me to believe. I picked up my water and took another drink. My hands weren't trembling now; they were shaking, making it difficult for me to drink without spilling water on myself.

"He," the attorney said, clearing his throat before continuing. "He, your uncle, killed your aunt with bacon grease?"

"Yes."

"That's unbelievable," he said, shaking his head. "What happened after that?"

Sighing, I closed my eyes and went back into the horror of my memory, the terror of that day.

"I tried to be quiet, so I wouldn't draw his attention – I didn't want him to use the bacon grease on me next. I watched as he cut the tape holding Aunt Tisha in the chair, letting her slump to the floor with a *thud*. He kept mumbling something about 'poor piggy.' He dragged her out the back door, onto the covered wooden porch; he left her lying there, with her feet still sticking though the doorway.

"I heard his heavy booted footsteps as he walked around on the porch, as if he was searching for something he couldn't find. He swore loudly, and then I saw him strolling toward the barn, just like he was going out to milk the cows; not hurried, but relaxed and enjoying the day.

"I tugged my wrists and legs gently, to see if there was any possibility of getting free, and the rope grew tighter and tighter against my throat. I could barely breathe; I tilted my head back and sucked in as much air as I could.

"I heard Uncle Troy's steps on the porch again, and watched out of the corner of my eye, as he moved around Aunt Tisha's body. I heard cloth ripping, and I saw her feet wiggle back and forth like she was being rolled over. Suddenly the feet disappeared.

"I saw Uncle Troy through the window, throwing a rope over top one of the beams that supported the porch roof; he tugged with all his weight. I could hear him grunting and swearing as he struggled with the rope. After a minute or two, I saw that he was hefting Aunt Tisha's naked body up to hang upside down. She was hung like the pigs, after they were slaughtered. More tears fell from my eyes. My teeth were chattering from my fear and dread. I didn't want to watch, but for some reason I couldn't look away and had to know what was happening – almost like if I saw everything he did, I would somehow find an advantage that might save me, even though every movement he made was more terrible than the last.

"He came back into the kitchen, glanced at me, and shook his head. 'You silly piglet, you're gonna hurt yourself,' he said. Coming over to where I was, he loosened the rope so I could breathe without my head being tilted back, but still tight enough that my back had to stay arched; my whole body was aching from the effort of staying in that position.

"Leaning down behind me, he whispered in my ear: 'I haven't forgotten about you. Don't worry, you're gonna be next.' He kissed the side of my neck. I closed my eyes and tried not to scream – I didn't want to give him the satisfaction.

"He turned and sorted through the knives in a wooden block on the counter, whistling under his breath. He must have found what he was looking for because he carried a couple of them outside with him.

"Turning my head, I saw him walking around Aunt Tisha's body, thoughtfully. He nodded, put one of the knives on a small table that was usually used to sit afternoon drinks on when we were relaxing on the porch. With the one he still held, he started cutting into Aunt Tisha's stomach, just like I'd seen him do when he was gutting a pig or a cow. He pulled out her guts, throwing them behind him, into the brilliant green grass of the yard; they landed with a sickening *plop*. Scarlet blood flew through the air, dripped from Uncle Troy's arms and streamed from Aunt Tisha's carcass.

"After he'd removed her guts, he changed to the other knife and slowly used it to cut off both her breasts, throwing them in the yard as well. He started cutting strips of skin and meat from Aunt Tisha's stomach, and these went onto the table along with both knives.

"He turned and walked off the porch again, this time around the side of the house. I heard the squeak of the outside faucet being turned on and soon I heard his boots on the porch again. He reappeared with the blue rubber water hose and began spraying Aunt Tisha as if she was nothing more than an animal that was needed to provide food. After she was rinsed, he rinsed the strips of meat he'd laid aside.

"When he was done, he put the hose away and turned off the water. He gathered up the knives, and the pieces, before coming back into the kitchen. He dumped his load into the sink, washed the knives, put them back into the block, and proceeded to wash his hands and get out a clean skillet. Placing it on the stove, he turned on the gas burner; he laid the strips of flesh into the skillet, just like bacon.

"I gagged at the smell that rose from his cooking. He turned at the sound and laughed. 'You don't like the smell, sweet piglet?' he asked sarcastically. 'It's just a pig frying in a skillet – just bacon. You like bacon.' I looked away, and tried hard not to throw up on myself, knowing if I did, I would probably strangle to death. Laughing again, Uncle Troy turned back to the stove.

"He switched on the radio and grabbed a fork from a drawer. He sang along to the country western songs, flipping his 'bacon' as it cooked. I closed my eyes, and prayed that he wouldn't kill me, that he wouldn't hurt me, and that this would end somehow, soon!

"Uncle Troy spilled some grease from his wife-bacon on the stove when he tried to drain it off, and it splattered on the floor; he swore, stepped around it, and continued to cook.

"When the wife-bacon was done, he put the strips on a paper towel to drain, and cooked himself two eggs in the same skillet. He plated his breakfast and sat at the table to eat, directly across from me. His eyes watched me as he ate slowly, seeming to enjoy every bite like you would slowly sip a fine wine. After watching him eat the first couple bites, I stared at the ceiling and tried to think about something else."

The attorney gagged. I looked at him and noticed he was actually turning a sickening shade of green.

"He ate her?" he asked.

I nodded.

"That's so. . .so. . ." He gagged again.

"Wrong?"

"Yes," he exclaimed. "How did you get away?"

I smiled gently and continued with my story.

"Uncle Troy sat and ate every bite of his breakfast – chewing and watching me. The look in his eyes gave me chills; I saw him watching my breasts as I tried to breathe and yet not move because of the rope. I closed my eyes so I wouldn't see him watching me, but it was almost worse somehow, because with my eyes closed all I could do was smell and hear – I smelled the aroma of what he'd cooked and I heard his fork clink off the plate as he took each bite.

"Eventually the clinking stopped. I opened my eyes as I heard the scraping of a kitchen chair on the hardwood floor. I watched as Uncle Troy took his plate to the sink and washed it, as well as the other dishes he'd dirtied. He dried them and put them away.

"He walked over beside me and began stroking my hair; leaning down he kissed my forehead. 'I'll be right back for you,' he said, and went outside again, to the barn. At least that was the direction I saw him go. When he reappeared in my line of vision through the window, I saw a silver metal bucket in his hand as he headed toward the pig pens.

"My mind was working a mile a minute, but I still couldn't think of a way to escape. I prayed again, for God to help me out of the mess I was in. I was just finishing my plea to God when I saw Uncle Troy again; he had mud smeared on his shirt and hands – the bucket was half covered with mud as well. I remember thinking: Mud? Why mud? But, I didn't have to wait long to find out.

"His boots thudded slowly on the porch and the screen door screeched as it opened. He stood there – in the doorway – staring at me for what felt like hours. I stared back, which seemed to excite him. He grinned and advanced into the room, walking around the table and over to where I sat. The bucket made a loud *thunk* as he sat it on the floor beside my chair. He knelt down in front of me and placed his hands on my knees, making me jump. He laughed.

"He squeezed my legs. I never realized he was so big – I'd never been so close to him before. One of his hands was big enough to cover my knee and half of my thigh. He didn't say anything for the longest time, but just kept squeezing and rubbing my legs, his breath coming faster and faster. I was trembling, not only from fear, but from the continued strain of my physical position; it had to have been over an hour since he'd tied me to the chair.

"Finally he said something: 'I'm gonna play nice with you, my sweet little piggy.' He dipped one of his hands into the bucket, scooping out a big handful of mud – at least I hoped it was mud, my nose had been burning ever since he'd made his breakfast, and I could no longer smell anything. He rubbed his hands together, caking them both with the thick, brown slime. He put his hands back on my legs and began to smear the filth from my knees to the edge of my shorts. I felt his fingers slip further and further under them each time. I was crying uncontrollably; sobs wracked my body and I felt the rope tightening, but I didn't care anymore, I just wanted it to be over.

"At some point he must have decided that my legs were brown enough, because he stopped, moved around to the back of the chair, and stood behind me – I could feel his breath against my neck as he bent toward me. He stuck out his tongue and licked from the base of my neck up to my ear. I gagged, jerking on the rope.

"He laughed and loosened the rope to keep me alive. Bending over, he got more mud from the bucket and started to massage it into my shoulders and around my neck, getting closer and closer to the neckline of my shirt. 'Squeal like a piggy for me, honey,' he growled in my ear. I jerked my head sideways and the rope tightened again. This time he didn't loosen it right away, but let me sputter and gag as he shoved his muddy hands down the front of my shirt. I started to black out and was thanking God for allowing me mercy, when he loosened the rope again.

"At that moment a truck pulled up in front of the house, drawing his attention to the living room windows; he swore and walked over to see who was there. I heard a truck door slam and heard him swear again. He turned, heading back toward me, passing by the stove. His boots were muddy and he slid in a bit of the grease that he'd spilled earlier. Grabbing a chair he righted himself, grinning. 'I'll be right back, my little piglet, to finish taking care of you,' he said. I cringed.

"He'd turned to go outside when he slipped again, going down this time. Both of his muddy, booted feet flew up, hitting the underside of the kitchen table. He twisted in the midair and his right temple hit the corner of the stove with a sickening crunch; he fell to the floor and didn't move."

Closing my eyes, I took a deep breath.

"Was he dead?" the attorney exclaimed. "When he hit his head. . . Did it kill him?"

I nodded as more tears slid down my face.

"A neighbor from the next farm over had come to see if Uncle Troy had a part for his tractor. You see, Uncle Troy and the neighbor had the same model and Uncle Troy had a couple of junk ones he kept for parts. When he didn't find Uncle Troy in the barn, he headed for the house. He spotted my aunt and came running. He came through the door and saw Uncle Troy on the floor, and me tied and gagged with mud all over; he untied me and removed the gag, before going to the phone and calling 9-1-1. He kept saying, 'Oh, Gawd! Oh, Lordie! Oh, Gawd!'

"By the time he'd untied me, and made the call, I'd passed out. I don't know if it was from exhaustion, relief, or trauma; it took me two weeks before I was able to tell the sheriff what had happened."

"Wow, that is terrible," the attorney said. "Two people were dead, and for what? Burnt bacon?"

I laughed harshly. "Yeah, burnt bacon. What a world, huh?"

The attorney sat there for a moment shaking his head, trying to wrap his mind around something that no sane human could ever understand.

"I don't get it," he said frowning. "What does that have to do with you being here now?"

I sighed.

"I was engaged to Mark, who was great. We were in love and he was considerate and romantic. A week before we were to be married, he told me that his favorite food was bacon and that he would like to have it every morning for breakfast. I was stunned. He went on to tell me how he would like it cooked and that I better not burn it, or I would be punished – then he laughed. If I would have thought about it a moment I would have known he was joking, or at least I would like to think I would have known. But it was too late.

"I walked into the kitchen and took out the biggest, sharpest knife we owned. I came back to the living room and stabbed him; I don't remember how many times. All I could think about was that day at the farm when Uncle Troy had killed my aunt and was about to rape me, all because of bacon. I guess I just lost it."

I pushed my hands into my hair, resting my forehead on my palms.

"Holy cow," the attorney whispered. "You killed him because he liked bacon? Because of your uncle and how he snapped because of bacon? This is almost too ludicrous! I've never had such a case before! Are you pulling my leg here? Because I really don't have time to be sent on a wild roller coaster of lies right now – I have a huge case load."

Dropping my hands, I looked at him with tears in my eyes.

"I knew you wouldn't believe me," I accused. "You want proof? Call this sheriff."

Grabbing his pen and a piece of his paper, I wrote down the name of the town and the sheriff who'd investigated the farm incident.

He took the piece of paper, read it, re-read it, and looked at me and blinked.

"I'll look into it," he said, stuffing his files and papers back into his leather briefcase. "If this is all true, we have a good chance of pleading temporary insanity."

I just sat there watching him; he was almost comical in his rush to get out of the cell.

"I'll be in touch," he said over his shoulder as he dashed out the door when the guard opened it.

I saw him lean toward the guard and say something; I didn't catch all that he said, but I heard the word bacon echo down the hall.

I threw my head back and laughed at the absurdity of it all. The death count was rising – three were dead on account of bacon.

EVIL MOUNTAIN

The darkness thickened as Hinun moved deeper into the forest. There was no sound except his steps and panting breath. He'd been on the trail for days, searching for his missing father, hoping that he'd find him alive, but with each passing day his hope slowly died.

Yesterday he'd found Father's bow. It had been lying beside a tree. The bow was broken, the wood splintered and scared with teeth marks. Hinun didn't know what might have made the marks, as they were large and deep, almost going completely through the handle of the long bow.

There had been blood on the string – dried blood, dark brown from the passage of time. If it had been red and wet Hinun would still have some expectancy of finding Father alive, but not now. It had been too long.

After searching for another day, finding nothing more, Hinun headed home. When he arrived, he would tell his mother and his sister that all hope was lost.

~ * ~

Kilna watched for her son's return. She was scared for him and for his father, whom he'd gone in search of. She'd been against the whole thing. If her husband wasn't coming back, she didn't see any point in risking her son as well.

She hung wet laundry out on the line – the thick woven cord scraping against her palms and chaffing her fingers. The cold wind that was blowing down from Evil Mountain didn't help. Winter would be upon them soon and they weren't ready. It seemed each year it was coming sooner. Everyone blamed the witch. She lived high in the snowy peaks of Evil Mountain, and she was evil herself. But she wasn't the only creature of evil intent that lived in that harsh environment. There were many strange beasts that dwelled there. That's how the mountain got its name.

Catching a movement by the path that lead to the forest, Kilna turned her head sharply, her heart leaping with hope. But, it fell again as she saw that it was only five-year-old Duna chasing a cat around the yard.

"Duna," Kilna called gently. "Don't play so close to the woods. It's not safe, darling."

Duna looked up, a defiant light in her dark blue eyes. "I want the kitty."

Kilna smiled. "Yes, I know you want the kitty, but I don't want you to get hurt."

Duna looked from her mother to the cat and huffed. She turned and stomped back into the yard, toward the cottage. She plopped her butt on the sandstone step in front of the door, crossed her arms, and huffed again.

Kilna bit back a grin as she watched her daughter pout. When she crossed her little arms and frowned like that, Duna looked like her father. Thinking of Jotan brought a frown to Kilna's brow as well. Questions swirled in her head: *Where is he? What happened to him? Why isn't Hinun back yet?*

Kilna and Duna feed the chickens, the goat, the cow, and the pig before heading to the cottage for the night. It was wise to be inside before dark, because no one knew what would be lurking in the shadows.

~ * ~

Hinun had made it halfway to his farm before he noticed. There was definitely something following him. But, whatever it was, it was staying far enough behind him that he couldn't see it.

When he started walking, he could hear shuffling behind him. He could hear low moans on the wind that sent shivers down his spine.

After crossing a shallow river, Hinun decided to see what was there, if anything. He sometimes thought it was his imagination playing tricks on him. There were many tales of men driven mad by spending too much time in the shadow of Evil Mountain.

He made his way up the steep, fern-covered bank, and paused as if looking for a deer path in the foliage in front of him, and heard a moan.

Without looking behind him, Hinun advanced into the forest, letting the branches of the trees hide him with their leaves. He walked a good ten yards before he hopped over a bush, off the path he'd been following, and circled back to the river. Whoever or whatever was following him had been keeping their distance, so he knew he had time.

Hinun sat between the roots of a large weeping willow a few yards up the bank from where he'd crossed earlier. The fronds cast enough shadows to conceal him, but they were far enough apart that he could see through them clearly.

Sitting still like he was hunting deer, he waited and watched, ignoring his body's discomfort.

He didn't have to wait long.

Not twenty minutes after sitting down, the brush on the opposite side of the bank began to shudder, like there was a strong breeze. There was no wind that day, so Hinun knew it for what it was. Something was out there, making it move.

He sat tense, holding his breath and drawing his bow, ready to let an arrow fly as soon as any threat presented itself.

A pale hand came through and held the bushes and ferns aside, as a hunched over man came stumbling out of the woods. His head was bent at an odd angle and he moaned and winced with each step.

Hinun watched the man stumble down the bank and fall into the water. He struggled to stand once again. Something about him was familiar. The clothes! Those were his father's clothes!

Pulling to full draw, Hinun almost let go of the bow string when the strange man turned and he got a glimpse of his face.

"Father," Hinun breathed, relaxing his shoulder. The bow went limp in his hands and the arrow fell to the sand at his feet.

He couldn't believe what he was seeing. His father was alive.

After the shock had passed, Hinun jumped up and went running, splashing through the water to his father.

"Father!" he yelled, throwing his arms around him.

~ * ~

Jotan didn't respond at first, when a young man embraced him with enthusiasm. His mind was cloudy. Ever since the battle, he hadn't been able to think straight. The strange wolf-man and the staggering ghoul had seemed to come out of nowhere and he wasn't at all prepared for what had happened next.

He'd just made camp for the night when the strange pair stepped into the light cast by his small cooking fire. He'd grabbed his bow and shot the ghoul, but it didn't seem to bother him, he just kept stepping drunkenly forward.

The wolf, standing on its back legs, at least ten feet tall, had taken his bow and broken it. Jotan had bent down to retrieve his hunting knife from his boot and the ghoulish creature had bitten him, ripping off a chunk of flesh.

He remembered stabbing the ghoul in the mouth with his blade as it dove for another bite; it had fallen limp and dead to the ground. But, there was still the werewolf, at least, that was what the thing appeared to be.

Jotan battled with the beast for a while, until loss of blood had made him weak. The dark grey creature had stood over him, roaring, and he'd expected to be eaten alive at any moment. But, instead, the werewolf had dropped down on all fours and sniffed him, growling deep in his throat.

A loud, high-pitched whistle had broken through the night air and the beast's head had jerked up. It howled, whimpered, and ran off toward the source of the sound.

Jotan had managed to crawl over to his bed roll and pass out, not expecting to see morning.

Strange memories of that night still flitted through his mind. Images that seemed like nothing more than dreams, of the wolf returning with a young, beautiful woman. She looked into his face and he'd seen into the dark depths of her cold black eyes. Somehow he'd known she was the witch that dwelled on the mountain.

"Ah," she'd said. "You've killed my pet. Don't worry – I'm not angry. You will soon prove useful."

She threw back her head and laughed. The dying embers of the fire created dancing lights in her black wavy hair, which made her look like she was surrounded with glittery magic.

He'd turned his head and had seen the werewolf standing on the other side of the waning fire, just watching.

He'd had a fever, so he'd thought it had all been his imagination, until he woke up the next morning in a haze, his body not wanting to move. There was a long black hair clinging to the front of his shirt, and he'd known that it had been real. He hadn't liked what that implied.

Now, here he was with some young man hugging him, calling him "father."

Jotan didn't recognize him, and it wouldn't have mattered if he did. He'd lost his ability to speak days ago. This strange sickness was doing weird things to his body.

The young man pulled back, letting him go. The world spun then clouded over. He landed in the water with a splash, unconscious.

~ * ~

Hinun gasped as Father fell into the water, face down. Quickly, he flipped him over before he could drown, and dragged him to the bank. Frantically, he tried to revive him, to no avail.

Laying Father's head down gently, Hinun went in search of something he could use to make a stretcher to move him on. He could drag him home, but not without a bit of help.

Twenty yards up the bank Hinun came across a couple of saplings that were tall enough and thick enough for what he had planned. It took him the rest of the day to cut them down with his small hand ax and lash them together with a coil of twine he had in his pack, and his cloak.

By the time he was ready to set off, it was almost dark. Hinun knew that if he pushed, and they didn't get caught up in the underbrush, they could make it home by morning. His concern for Father's life was urging him to risk the dangers of traveling at night, in the shadow of Evil Mountain.

~ * ~

"What do you mean you can't find him?" Freka yelled at Yito. "Do I have to do everything myself?"

The witch slammed her fist down on the arm of her huge wooden chair with such fury that the werewolf flinched. He wouldn't turn again until the moon rose, and he wished it would hurry up and happen. Yito wanted out of her presence and out in the freedom of the woods.

Yito bowed. "I'm sorry I've disappointed you, mistress."

"Disappointed me?" Freka asked with a snarl. "You've done far more than disappoint me. You've shown how useless and incompetent you really are! I should kill you right now!"

Freka raised her hand and the blood ruby in her ring glowing ominously on her finger.

Yito threw himself at her feet. "Please no! I'll do anything for you, mistress, anything. Please let me live."

He was strong and formidable in werewolf form, but as a man he was skinny and frail. He hated the weakness of his human body and wanted to be a werewolf all the time. Freka had the power to make it happen, but she would only give him what he wanted if he served her well. He had to make this up to her or she would never give him that gift.

"I know where the man's family lives," Yito lied. "I can go there tonight and bring him back here for you. I can!"

Freka lowered her hand and the ruby lost half of its radiance. "Get up. I hate it when you grovel like a dog."

Yito slowly rose to his feet, careful not to touch her feet. Last time he'd accidently bumped into her, she'd had him beaten. The scars on his back were the reminder of the brutality of her lover, Lendor.

The vampire had delighted in beating him, jealous of the time and attention that Freka gave him. But Yito knew it was because she wanted to manipulate him, both of them probably. She loved to pit them against each other.

Freka stood and walked around Yito, looking him over.

He felt her fingernails slide through the white grooves on his back as she walked.

"You won't disappoint me again, will you?" she asked playfully.

"No, mistress," Yito said, hearing the steel undertone in her flirtatious purr. "I'll never disappoint you again."

"Good," she chirped with a smile. "I want you to bring him, and his entire family, and I want them all here by midnight. Lendor needs to feed. They should make quite a banquet for him."

Yito bowed. "Yes, mistress, as you wish."

He turned to leave and had almost made it out the door when she called after him.

"Yito!"

He turned and bowed. "Yes, mistress?"

"If you succeed, I'll give you what you want. If you don't, you'll die."

Yito bowed again, turned, and left. He didn't know how he was going to find out where the family was and get them back before midnight, but he knew he'd die trying. He was as good as dead anyway if he failed. He had nothing to lose.

~ * ~

Hinun dragged Father through the woods. It was almost pitch black, with the trees blocking out any and all light. He'd stumbled numerous times, scraping his knee, and cutting his palm. Not being able to see where he was going was also causing the stretcher to get stuck where the poles dragged the ground. At this rate they wouldn't make it home by morning.

He sat down to rest for a moment, his entire body covered in sweat from exertion. Gently setting down the poles he'd been dragging, he flopped to the ground and lay still, just breathing in the cool night air. Before he realized it, he fell asleep.

~ * ~

Kilna had just tucked a sleeping Duna into her small cot close to the fire when she heard it: howling on the wind. It waft through the open window and to her ears as the stench of a skunk would have come to her nose.

She shivered as she walked over to the window, expecting some dark creature intent on harm to be standing there, waiting to grab her and drag her through.

No one was there. The yard was empty. There wasn't so much as a racoon looking for stray bits of chicken feed. The night was silent – too silent.

Gripping the rough wood of the shutters, Kilna closed the window and slid the board into place to keep it shut.

She undressed and went to bed, praying that the men she so dearly loved were safe.

If she'd waited a moment longer before shutting the window, she'd have seen a two-headed dragon in the sky, silhouetted by the moon, with a werewolf on its back. Then she would have realized that no amount of praying would keep Hinun and Jotan safe that night.

~ * ~

Hinun woke with a start. Father was awake and was thrashing around, trying to get free of the stretcher. He'd lashed him down with their leather belts, so he wouldn't fall out and get hurt.

"Father?" Hinun called out, getting up off the ground. "I fell asleep. Are you all right?"

As he stepped closer, Father strained against the leather and snapped at Hinun, like he was trying to bite him.

"Father, what's wrong?" Hinun asked, reaching forward to feel Jotan's head.

Jotan lunged for the juicy sticks of meat, trying to bite them off.

Hinun pulled his hand back quickly, not understanding what was going on. "Are you hungry? I have some jerky in my pack."

After retrieving the jerky he held it up to Father's mouth, but he cocked his head and tried to bite Hinun's hand again.

Frowning, Hinun tucked the jerky away and picked up the poles, continuing home. While he was walking, he contemplated his father's strange behavior, unaware of the threat that hovered just above the trees.

~ * ~

Yito had decided that Gox was his best bet of finding the man and his family, and transporting them back to the ice castle alive. There was no way he could do it himself.

Glancing at the moon, he estimated the time to be somewhere around ten o'clock. That left him two hours to accomplish his mission, and four hours before the potion Freka had given him to make his change would wear off.

Gox had been surprisingly compliant. Normally the two headed dragon would baulk at letting Yito ride him, but he hadn't been out in a while and seemed eager to fly, even if it was with his least favorite passenger.

Yito watched the heads of the dragon swing back and forth in the wind. One would breathe fire one minute, and the other would spew ice the next. Gox seemed to be playing, and that was fine with Yito, as long as it didn't interfere with his mission. So far things were going great.

He'd already managed to spot the infected man in the woods. His scent was unmistakable. As his body changed from human to zombie, he began to stink in a way that no other creature could. But Yito smelled fresh blood with him as well. This confused him. He didn't know why the new zombie hadn't attacked and fed yet. But, he wasn't going to make them aware of his presence just to see why. That could wait. He just hoped that they were leading them to more people. Family or not, he had to show up at midnight with a few humans if he wanted to be rewarded.

~ * ~

Hinun looked up at the moon as he dragged his father the last few feet into the yard. It was after eleven. He just hoped Mother would open the door for him. Crawling through the yard, every muscle in his body protesting even the slightest movement, he made his way to the door.

Knocking with all the strength he had left, Hinun passed out on the step.

~ * ~

Kilna heard a thumping on the door and jumped out of bed. Her hand flew to the latch, ready to tear it away, but caution made her pause. Pressing her ear to the door, she stood silently waiting for a sound to come to her, telling her who might be outside.

She heard a distant moan. It was almost too faint for her to perceive, but it was there all the same. Convinced that someone was hurt, she threw the door open and gasped at the prone body of her son on the door step.

Kneeling down, she cradled his head in her lap, slapping his cheeks.

"Wake up, Hinun," she pleaded.

He moaned, looked up into his mother's face, and smiled. "Mother."

She leaned forward and kissed his forehead. "Shh. We can talk when you've rested."

Hinun's brow wrinkled in a frown and he tried to sit up. "No, Father!"

Kilna frowned down at her son, applying pressure to his shoulder to still his movements and urge him to again relax. "What about Jotan? Where is he?"

Hinun lifted his arm and pointed to the edge of the yard, where he'd left the stretcher.

Kilna jumped up, careful not to let Hinun's head fall on the hard stone, and ran to her husband. Her long white cotton nightgown plastered itself to her body and slowed her down, but she was still there in a couple of seconds.

The stretcher was empty. Lifting the straps she noted that they had teeth marks on them; they'd been chewed through.

She turned back to the cottage to see a two headed dragon standing beside it, and a werewolf throwing Hinun's body over its neck. She dropped the straps and screamed, running to her son's aid.

She'd only gone five feet when a shadow fell over her – the shadow of her husband.

"Jotan?" she whispered. "Jotan!"

She threw herself into his arms, too happy and excited at seeing him alive to stop herself. Pulling back, she looked up into his eyes – vacant eyes, cloudy eyes. She shivered and pulled away.

Jotan moaned and stepped toward her, gripping her arm, dragging her back to him. With his other hand he pulled her hair violently, lowering his wide-open mouth to her neck. He was about to sink his teeth into her soft warm flesh when something slammed into the side of his head, knocking him down.

While Jotan was shaking his head and trying to figure out where the meal that had just been in his arms had gone, Yito knocked Kilna out and carried her to the dragon.

Jotan struggled to his feet slowly, sniffing the air to see if he could locate the food that he knew was around. A strange smell entered his nostrils. It was stronger than human scent, and more musky. Staggering slowly, Jotan made his way toward the strange smell, wondering if whatever it was, would be a good meal.

Yito went into the small cottage and stood over the cot of a little girl, and just looked at her. He could smell her sweet innocence and wanted to sink his teeth into her, rip her apart, and savor every drop of her blood. But, he knew that if he did Freka and Lendor would kill him. He had to restrain himself and take her with him. There would be other innocent humans to enjoy later.

Yito picked her up, careful not to wake her, and turned toward the door.

The zombie was standing there pretending to look around. Yito knew he couldn't see anything; the last one had been completely blind and had traveled through life depending completely on scent. He assumed this one was the same.

Yito took a step forward and the zombie grunted and stepped inside.

Walking forward with purpose, Yito lifted one of his rear legs off the ground and kicked the zombie in the gut, sending him flying through the air to land in the dirt of the yard. He was extremely careful not to jar the child or to make a sound. He didn't want to accidently kill her when he tried to knock her out. He wanted her to stay asleep as long as possible.

Jotan grunted and groaned, rolling all over the yard, trying to get up, not realizing that his leg was broken.

Yito shook his massive wolf head at the zombie. He couldn't believe how stupid they were. No brain power, just driven by blood lust. He didn't understand what Freka kept one around for.

Shrugging, Yito tied the girl to her mother, making sure the bonds were tight enough that if she woke up and struggled, that he wouldn't lose her.

Gox raised his heads as Yito mounted. Growling, he nodded toward the zombie still rolling around in the yard. Gox huffed smoke and snow and took flight, grabbing the zombie in his claws as they took to the air.

Yito was excited. He'd done what he'd said he could do. He'd gotten the zombie and the family. Finally, he would be granted his wish. He would be a werewolf all the time.

As they flew to the ice castle, he dreamed about what it would feel like to have sunshine on his fur as he frolicked through the woods.

~ * ~

Freka was waiting expectantly at the door when they arrived.

"I'm impressed," she said, looking over the cargo. "I didn't expect you to deliver. Lendor will be pleased."

Yito growled contentedly, pleased with his mistress' approval.

"After Lendor feeds," Freka purred. "I'll give you what I promised."

Yito nodded and set about unloading the cargo. The little girl had woken up during the flight and had screamed for a while, but now she was silent and ridged. He was sure she was in shock.

"Yito," Freka said. "Would you tie up the zombie for me? Just chain him to the wall or something – anything to keep him out of the way for now."

Yito grunted, acknowledging the request.

Freka lifted her hand, the ruby glowing bright, and mumbled something under her breath; and the humans stood and lined up in a row, facing forward.

"Walk," she said, and they walked.

Yito watched for a moment, always amazed at the witch's power, before he grabbed the zombie by the scruff of the neck and hauled him off to tie him up.

~ * ~

Lendor stood at the window, staring out into the darkness with his arms folded behind his back as Freka brought in the humans. He turned to survey his gift.

"Not bad," he said, walking toward them. "I had hoped for the girl to be older, but I can't have everything now, can I?"

Freka frowned. "Why did you want the girl to be older?"

"Ah, my darling, I don't see why you like to ask such silly questions," he said as he examined Kilna.

"What's that supposed to mean?" Freka snapped. "If you don't stop talking in riddles, I'll let the zombie and the werewolf have them and you'll have to hunt your own food."

Lendor turned to look at the witch, hissed, and bore his teeth.

She shrank back. "You're grumpy. You need to feed. I'll go and make sure our new zombie is settling in."

Freka hurried to leave. Lendor sometimes scared her. He was the only one that wasn't afraid of her powers. In truth, they didn't work on him at all for some reason. She could do as she wanted with everyone else, but not with him, which was why he was her lover; it excited her to have someone that she couldn't control.

Yito had done what he was asked. The zombie was chained to the wall in the cellar, a collar connecting him to the wall. He was in bad shape though, with a broken leg, and his guts hanging out of a gash that Gox's claws had made.

She sighed and headed back upstairs to see how Lendor's feeding was going.

Freka opened the door and stepped into the lounge, stopping dead in her tracks at what she saw.

Lendor had already feed on the young man – the limp body was lying on the floor where he'd been standing. The young girl was still standing where she'd been earlier, staring off into space, but that wasn't what had caught Freka's attention.

It was the woman. Lendor had her bare to the waist, kneeling in front of him. His mouth was attached to her neck where he slowly sucked the blood from her body while he caressed her torso. The woman was gasping and panting. He was taking his time with her and enjoying her as more than just a meal. He was enjoying her as a woman as well.

Freka gasped as a red-hot ball of jealousy shot through her body. Stomping over to the couple, she grabbed the woman's head and, with a twist, broke her neck, killing her instantly.

Lendor reared back and hissed. He was angry that his main course had been taken from him before he was ready. Closing his eyes, he licked his lips, savoring the last taste of the woman before the blood went cold.

Standing, he loomed over Freka.

"What did you do that for?" Lendor growled.

"You were touching her," Freka screamed. "Enjoying her!"

"Yes, I was enjoying her," he said. "You gave her to me to enjoy, didn't you?"

"Not like that," Freka huffed. "To feed, not to fondle!"

Lendor's hand shot out and gripped Freka's neck, lifting her off the floor and cutting off her air.

"I have no need of a jealous woman," he snapped. "I won't be controlled by you or anyone else. If I want to enjoy another woman, I will, and there is nothing you can do about it."

He dropped Freka to the ice floor and stomped over to the little girl. Grabbing her, he bit her neck and sucked the life out of her. Dropping her limp body, he wiped blood off his mouth with the back of his hand and turned to leave the room.

Freka gasped for breath, her anger growing with every intake of air. *How dare he act this way?!* she thought, her rage building. *How dare he treat me like any normal woman?!* Standing, she raised her hand and slammed the door shut in front of him, her ring glowing so bright that the entire room was red.

Lendor bowed his head for a moment before he turned. Facing her, he looked her straight in the eye and walked toward her. He stopped when they were six inches from each other – his eyes were ablaze with an anger equal to her own.

"Open the door," he said in a low menacing voice. "I'm not in the mood to play your games."

Freka didn't say anything. She just stared back at him.

Before she knew what was happening, Lendor grabbed her head, jerked it to the side, and bit into her neck.

She clawed at his face, tried to push him away, crying out in pain and fear.

He tightened his grip the more she fought.

Gradually the light in her ring faded and went out. Her arms hung limp at her sides.

Lendor dropped her dead body to the floor, and left the room. He stopped suddenly in the hall as he felt the castle shudder around him. From below, he heard the howl of a werewolf, the moans of a zombie, and the thundering roar of a dragon. Something occurred to him, but it was too late. Freka must have had all the beasts under her control. Now there was nothing to stop them from tearing him apart. Quickly, he headed for the main entrance of the castle, but not quickly enough.

~ * ~

Gox roared as a black fog cleared from his mind. The walls surrounding him made him feel hemmed in and uncomfortable. He thrashed around and his tail hit the chain that held Jotan the zombie to the wall, freeing him to roam the ice castle.

Rearing up, Gox's heads hit the ceiling above him, breaking through. His fire head became stuck and he tugged it back down frantically, trying to free himself. He shot fire and ice all around, hitting everything. Flames sizzled as they fought with ice.

Finally freeing his head, Gox pulled down a large chunk of the frozen floor, and Lendor with it. Knocking him out as he landed in the cellar.

~ * ~

Jotan moaned and shuffled around, not really aware of the danger he was in from the thrashing Gox. Sniffing the air, he smelled blood – human blood.

Slowly, he hobbled toward what his nose told him was food. He fell on top of the prone body of a weird smelling man. Following his nose, Jotan found the human blood he'd smelled, all over Lendor's neck and hands. He licked the body, confused by the smell of the vampire. When the human blood he'd licked off turned out to be what he thought it was, he dug right in, biting Lendor's neck and tearing it wide open.

Lendor came to screaming. He looked at the zombie who was happily munching on him and hissed, which didn't faze Jotan a bit as he went in for another bite.

The vampire lunged forward and ripped Jotan's head off, throwing it against the wall as hard as he could, and rolling out of the way of Gox's tail that was whizzing through the air toward him.

Standing, Lendor clutched his bleeding neck, glancing at the head of the zombie that was now rolling around on the ground, dented, but still chewing. He headed for the exit that was across the room, dogging Gox as he slashed, butted, and slammed into everything around him. Chunks of wall and ceiling were raining down like giant hail.

Just as Lendor reached the doorway, Yito appeared in the opening with a menacing growl, blocking his path.

The vampire hissed, and the werewolf snarled as they stood looking deep into each other's eyes, waiting for the other to make the first move.

Lendor, tired off all the chaos, lunged forward to grab Yito's neck.

Yito dropped down on all fours, avoiding Lendor's grasp and bit into the vampire's leg, sinking his teeth to the bone.

Lendor shrieked, cupped his hands like claws, and thrust them into Yito's back, grabbing his spine with both hands. With a sharp upward yank, he removed the spine from the neck down, leaving it dangling outside Yito's body.

Yito screamed and groaned in pain, but he didn't let go. His head was the only part of his body still functioning and he wasn't going to give up easily.

Lendor reached down and took hold of Yito's powerful jaws, pulling as hard as he could.

Yito growled.

Lendor groaned from the effort, but finally Yito's jaw gave way with a snap.

Yito yelped and moved no more, now just a dead lump of fur.

Lendor bent over to examine the damage to his leg and while he was distracted, Gox finally tore a hole in the wall big enough for him to escape.

Gox threw aside the last chunk of the ice wall, which landed on Lendor, knocking him over and pinning him to the floor. With a jumping leap the dragon perched for a moment in the opening, breathing in the predawn air, his tail slamming into the floor, gouging it in his excitement and freedom. He didn't notice Lendor, and didn't see that he had chopped him to bits, killing the vampire that he had once seen as master.

With a final roar of freedom, Gox took flight, spinning and weaving through the air, traveling far from Evil Mountain where "the evil" now lay dead in a crimson lake of blood.

THE HEART OF HEROISM

"Take that crap off!" Mr. Harper yelled. "Why are you always dressing up in stupid outfits? If I ever catch you out wearing something like that, I'm gonna burn all of your comic books! Every last, damn one!"

"S. . .s. . .sorry, Dad," Billy Jack said, pouting as he shuffled back to his bedroom. He stopped just inside the door and looked at himself in his mirror. The aluminum foil he'd used to make a lightning bolt on the chest of his red flannel union suit twinkled in the overhead light and made him smile with delight. He giggled. Running his hands over the B and J he'd cut out of stick-on felt and applied to the suit on either side of the bolt, he imagined himself as a real live superhero. "Super Billy Jack," he sighed.

"Hurry up!" his dad yelled. "We have work to do and I don't have time for any of your shit!"

Billy Jack's bottom lip quivered and tears welled up in his big, blue eyes as he peeled his costume off and slipped on a worn, stained pair of blue jeans and a plain, dark blue T-shirt; the cloth of the T-shirt stretched to its limits over the bulky muscles of his chest. He sniffed loudly, looked at himself in the mirror again, and rubbed his eyes with his knuckles like an upset toddler.

"Are you ready yet, you dumb oaf?" his dad yelled.

"Y. . .y. . .yes," Billy Jack answered and hurried back out to the living room of their tiny, basement apartment. "I'm ready to w. . .w. . .work. What's broken t. . .t. . .today?"

His father didn't answer right away. He just stared up at his mammoth son who towered over him with his six foot, four-inch height.

"Were you crying?" he asked Billy Jack. "Were you crying like a little sissy baby again?"

Billy Jack bit his lip and shook his head, fidgeting with the front of his shirt, stretching it to the point that the material was see through.

"Yes, you were," his dad said, scowling. "You have to quit acting like that, and you have to quit dressing up in those prissy outfits. Do you want people to make fun of you?"

Billy Jack sniffled and twisted his shirt nervously. "N. . .n. . .no. I just want to b. . .b. . .be a superhero."

Mr. Harper growled and ran a hand over his balding head. "You're never going to be a superhero! You're just a stupid nobody and always will be!" He sighed and shook his head. "Get your tool box. We have some plumbing to fix on the ninth floor."

"The n. . .n. . .ninth?" Billy Jack asked, letting go of his shirt and knuckling his eyes again. "Can I v. . .v. . .visit Mike? He's my bestest friend in the w. . .w. . .world."

Mr. Harper groaned. "Yeah, you can visit your friend if you do a good job, but if you give me any trouble, you won't be allowed." He yanked open the door to their apartment and stomped out into the hall, throwing an impatient glance back at his son.

Billy Jack shuffled forward and lifted the red, four drawer tool box sitting beside the door without much effort at all. He rushed out into the hall, following his dad, almost tripping himself in his hurry.

"Shut the door!" his dad hollered over his shoulder, stomping down the hall toward the elevator.

"O. . .o. . .okay, sorry," Billy Jack mumbled and turned, shutting the door before advancing down the hall as fast as he could. Without noticing, he started fidgeting with the hem of his shirt, twisting and tugging it out of proportion. Just as he reached the elevator, where his dad was waiting, the cold, metal door slid open with a dull ding.

"Up we g. . .g. . .go!" Billy Jack said, grinning. "Can I push the b. . .b. . .button, Dad?"

Mr. Harper sighed. "Sure." He stepped inside without looking at his son and slumped against the back wall.

"Yeah!" Billy Jack screamed, practically bouncing into the elevator. He pressed the appropriate button – the one with an L on it for "lobby"; there would get off there and use the stairs the rest of the way. There were other elevators in the building leading higher, but most of them were out of service because the building owner didn't consider fixing them worth the money. Mr. Harper always referred to him as a "Slum Lord."

In just a few seconds the door was dinging open to present the small, dingy, poorly lit lobby. It held the tenants little, square mailboxes along the far wall, which were covered in gang graffiti. Billy Jack thought it was beautiful and mystical, appearing out of nowhere after he'd scrub it off once a month. He imagined something magical lived inside the bank of mailboxes and that it would reveal itself a little at a time. When he washed it, he pretended the turpentine he used was a drug that put it to sleep for a time. Today, it was freshly painted with bright green and orange spray paint.

"The b. . .b. . .beast is awake," he whispered and stepped out of the elevator cautiously, pressing his body tight against the wall, watching the mailboxes across from him like they were going to swallow him alive.

Mr. Harper rolled his eyes and stepped out of the elevator, shaking his head. He ignored Billy Jack and walked to the stairwell, opened the door, and went inside, letting the door swing closed behind him.

"No!" Billy Jack screamed and ran forward, ripping the door open and entering the stairwell too, pulling the door tightly shut behind himself, breathing heavily.

His dad laughed and ascended the first flight of stairs.

"It's n. . .n. . .not funny, Dad," Billy Jack pouted. "You'd f. . .f. . .feel bad if the monster a. . .a. . .ate me."

"I would miss you so," his dad responded sarcastically.

Billy Jack smiled, thinking his dad really meant it and hurried up the stairs after him. "Who's p. . .p. . .plumbing is broken?"

Mr. Harper sighed. "Mrs. Willis' again."

"She's a n. . .n. . .nice lady," Billy Jack said, struggling with the tool box in the narrow stairwell, but keeping up nonetheless. "S. . .s. . .she makes good cookies."

"Yes, she does," his dad replied absently, limping slightly. He'd injured his knee when he was younger and it bothered him more and more as he grew older, and having to traverse many flights of stairs on a daily basis didn't help either. The pain it caused made him wish he was sitting downstairs in his recliner, drinking beer.

They made it to the landing of the fifth floor and Mr. Harper inwardly groaned. It was the one with the different colored tiles, because he'd had to replace some a few years back. He braced himself for what he knew was coming.

"Dad!" Billy Jack cried out. "Be c. . .c. . .careful! Only step on the white and b. . .b. . .blue tiles. The red o. . .o. . .ones will wake the d. . .d. . .dragon!"

Mr. Harper growled and marched around to his right to the next flight of stairs. Behind him he could hear the metallic rattle of the tools in the tool box as Billy Jack bounced it while trying to hop from one small square to another, missing the red ones that made up most of the floor; he reached the stairs with a sigh of relief.

"Dad, y. . .y. . .you should be more careful," Billy Jack admonished with solemn eyes. "S. . .s. . .someday the dragon m. . .m. . .might get you. You're l. . .l. . .lucky I know the r. . .r. . .right tile combination to l. . .l. . .lock his cage back up."

"It's thoughtful of you to save my life," his dad said, and continued to climb, wincing in pain as his limp became more pronounced.

They made it to the ninth floor of the "castle" as Billy Jack called it. It was easier for his mind to wrap itself around the occurrences and the strange people in his living environment to think of it that way. He pretended the building was a cursed castle and that he was the only one who would know how to save it when the curse became too strong for everyone else. Super Billy Jack would save the day! He didn't realize that he lived in the middle of the slums and most people living in the building were drug dealers, users, or prostitutes, and that was why they acted the way they did.

Mrs. Willis' plumbing didn't take long to fix and soon Billy Jack was standing outside apartment 947, waiting for someone to answer his insistent knock. He fidgeted with his shirt, twisting it this way and that while he glanced at the hall around him, imagining all kinds of sinister things lurking in the shadows.

He jumped when the door opened.

"Oh, it's you," a woman with ratty hair, smeared makeup, and a cigarette in her hand said. "Mike! Your friend's here to see you!" she screamed as smoke waft from her nose and mouth; she walked away, leaving the door standing wide open.

Billy Jack smiled nervously, still glancing around him and twisting his shirt. But Mike's little, smiling face appeared from around the corner and his fear melted away.

"Billy Jack," the five-year-old boy squealed, and wrapped his arms around Billy Jack's leg, hugging it tight in his skinny arms. He looks up at his big friend hopefully. "Did you come to play?"

He nodded and let the little boy pull him inside by his pant leg, shutting the door quickly behind them to keep the monsters out.

"I w. . .w. . .was a good w. . .w. . .worker today," Billy Jack said. "So, I was a. . .a. . .allowed to come and v. . .v. . .visit you!"

"Goodie," Mike said cheerfully. "I have a new toy!"

"Really?" Billy Jack asked. "What i. . .i. . .is it?"

"I show you!" Mike squealed, and darted toward his bedroom with his big friend trailing after him.

Billy Jack made it to the door to see Mike proudly holding two small plastic boxes with thick, black wires sticking out of the tops.

"Walk-me, talk-mes!" Mike yelled, waving them at Billy Jack. "My daddy gave them to me. He came to see me."

"Th. . .th. . .those are very nice," Billy Jack said solemnly. "What d. . .d. . .do they do?"

"I show you," Mike said, sitting on the edge of the bed and twisting the knobs on the tops of the plastic boxes causing brief bursts of static noise to come from each of them; he handed one to Billy Jack. "You sit!" he ordered, and pointed to his bed as he stood. "I'll hide in the closet."

"Okay," Billy Jack said, sitting on the edge of Mike's tiny bed; it groaned under his two hundred plus pounds.

Mike giggled and darted across his room and into his closet, closing the door behind him. "Test, test, one, two, three. . ."

Billy Jack jumped as Mike's voice came blaring out of the plastic box in his hand. He held it closer to his face, almost pressing his nose against it while he took a better look at the device. "H. . .h. . .how'd you get i. . .i. . .in there, Mike?" he asked the part with the little holes and heard a giggle come from the closet.

Mike opened the door and peered out at Billy Jack with a broad smile on his face. "I not in it, silly. I do this!" He pressed down the button on the side of the plastic box and talked into it again, rubbing his lips on the speaker because he was holding it too close to his mouth. "Test, test, one, two, three. . ." He giggled again and shut the door, hiding once more. "You do it! You do it!" came out of the box Billy Jack held.

He grinned and pressed down the button, holding the walkie-talkie close to his mouth. "H. . .h. . .i there, Mike. How's th. . .th. . .things in the closet?"

Mike squealed with laughter.

They played for hours, taking turns going into the closet and outside the bedroom, talking to each other through their own secret system.

Billy Jack was stepping back into Mike's room after his turn in the hall when he spotted the clock on the dresser. He gasped.

"Oh, n. . .n. . .no!" he exclaimed. "I'm l. . .l. . .late! My dad is going to be m. . .m. . .mad. I have to g. . .g. . .go. B. . .b. . .bye, Mike!"

He turned and rushed down the short hallway and out of the apartment. The halls and stairwells were dark in the early evening; the light coming through the barred window on each level was weak. Multiple times he tripped and almost fell down the stairs, but caught himself at the last moment with a cry of alarm. A few people were in the stairwell, a couple with guns and suitcases, but he just pushed past them, focused on getting home. He ignored their shouts of "Watch where you're going, dummy!" and kept on running.

By the time he reached the basement, he was whimpering and tugging on the front of his shirt with both hands, twisting it nervously. He was so focused on getting home that he didn't even notice he was tearing the shirt apart at the seams.

Finally his hand reached out and gripped the doorknob, trying to turn it. It didn't move. He cried out and then whimpered repeatedly trying harder to turn the knob.

The door suddenly flew open to reveal his dad standing there in a white tank top and his jeans, with a beer in his hand.

"Did you get lost?" he sneered as he lifted the bottle and took a deep swill of beer.

"N. . .n. . .no, Dad," Billy Jack muttered, looking down at the floor, tugging at his shirt. "I took t. . .t. . .too long and am l. . .l. . .late. I'm s. . .s. . .sorry."

Mr. Harper watched his son for a moment. "Where's the tool box? You were supposed to bring it back down with you."

Billy Jack went still for a moment with a shocked/scared expression on his face. "I f. . .f. . .forgot."

"Well, you better go back up there and get it," his dad growled, "because you aren't coming in here without it!" He stepped back and slammed the door in his son's face.

Tears poured from Billy Jack's eyes as he staggered back down the hall and toward the elevator. He pressed the button with no pleasure; his dad was mad at him and he was drinking, which was never a good combination. Gasping for breath between sobs, he climbed back onto the elevator and rode up to the lobby. From there his journey was uneventful and he didn't even play his game on the fifth floor landing.

He was still crying when he reached Mrs. Willis' apartment, and she answered shortly after his first knock.

"Billy Jack, I was wondering if you were coming back for the tool box," she said. "Why are you cryin', honey?"

"I f. . .f. . .forgot to come get the t. . .t. . .tool box and was l. . .l. . .late going home," he said, sniffling loudly. "Dad i. . .i. . .is mad at m. . .m. . .me."

"Ah, honey," she said, stepping forward to give him a hug. "It'll be all right. I have your tool box right here and you'll soon be home all safe and sound. Your daddy was probably just worried about you."

Billy Jack whimpered and hugged the woman back, loving the way it felt to have someone care about him.

"Th. . .th. . .thank you, Mrs. Willis," he said, sniffling again and stepping back. "I h. . .h. . .have to go now, b. . .b. . .before Dad gets more a. . .a. . .angry."

She patted his cheek and smiled, letting him step inside and retrieve the tool box that was sitting out of the way in the kitchen. "You be careful going back downstairs," she said as he left. "There's some mean folks around here and they would take advantage of a sweet, handsome boy like you."

"I w. . .w. . .will," he said, wiping the last of the tears from his face. "G. . .g. . .good night, Mrs. Willis."

"Good night, honey," she said, smiling as she closed the door behind him.

When the door clicked shut Billy Jack felt alone and scared. Not of the people Mrs. Willis had mentioned, but of his dad and what he would do for punishment; Billy Jack never liked his punishments.

He descended the stairs slower this time, dreading going home now. Watching every step as he went down in the now almost completely dark stairwell, he felt something hit his foot on the third floor landing, where he'd bumped into the angry men earlier in his rush. He bent down and felt around on the floor with his hand and found a smooth, squareish object. He picked it up and held it close to his face, squinting to see. It was one of Mike's walkie-talkies! He frowned, wondering how it had gotten there and realized after a few moments that he'd left Mike's apartment with it and must have dropped it when he bumped into the men.

He turned around and thought about taking it back to Mike's, but shook his head. It was too late now, Mike would be in bed, and Mike's mom scared him; she was mean when Billy Jack showed up too late or she didn't want him around. With a shrug he decided to take it home with him and give it back the next day.

Turning, he continued his descent and soon reached the basement once again. He trudged down the hall, now tired from going up and down the stairs so many times. Without even trying the knob on the door, he knocked, knowing from experience that it was locked; it was ripped open instantly.

His dad stood there once again, but this time he was swaying slightly and holding onto the door for support. He glanced down at the tool box Billy Jack was carrying.

"Tool box, good," he said, and staggered backwards, almost falling on the floor.

Billy Jack didn't say anything. He just stepped inside and sat the tool box by the door where it always sat when not in use. He closed the door and locked it and then went to his room, noticing as he left the living room that his dad had made it to his recliner in front of the TV, which was on; he sighed and opened another beer.

Flipping his light on, Billy Jack noticed right away that the shelf in his bedroom – across from the door – was empty. His comic books were gone! His heart started pounding and his hands started shaking. He grabbed a hold of his already mutilated shirt and tugged on it hard; the sound of it ripping fell on deaf ears, going unnoticed.

"Dad!" he cried, running back out to the living room. "Someone t. . .t. . .took my c. . .c. . .comic books!"

His dad laughed, looking over and up at his son with a smirk. "Yeah, I did," he said. "You were late and you didn't bring the tool box, so I burned them." He shrugged drunkenly and turned his attention back to the TV.

"N. . .n. . .no!" Booby Jim screamed at the top of his lungs, tugging his shirt at the same time, ripping it off of his body. He started crying and couldn't talk. Turning abruptly, he ran into his room, slammed the door behind him, and threw himself on his bed, sobbing hysterically.

He lay that way for almost an hour, with his huge body shaking from sobs, but finally fell asleep.

~ * ~

A loud noise woke Billy Jack suddenly and he blinked in confusion at the brightness of his room; he rolled over to see that the light was still on. From beyond his door he heard thumping and his dad screaming. Quickly, he got up and went to investigate.

"Dad are y. . .y. . .you okay?" he asked tentatively, still timid after what had happened earlier that evening.

His dad didn't answer, but he could hear low growling/grunting noises and when he turned the corner to get a view of the living room he saw the source. A strange man was kneeling over the prone body of his dad, feasting upon his guts; his face was buried deep in Mr. Harper's stomach.

"What are y. . .y. . .you doing to my d. . .d. . .dad?" he yelled, his hands balling into fists.

The man turned and looked in Billy Jack's direction with cloudy eyes; he hissed at Billy Jack and went back to eating.

"S. . .s. . .stop!" Billy Jack yelled, and stepped forward, kicking the strange man in the stomach, knocking him over and away from his dad and into the open apartment door, slamming it shut.

The man roared in anger, sending drops of blood flying from his lips and teeth. He charged at Billy Jack with his hands raised and his fingers bent into claws.

"No!" Billy Jack screamed, and punched the man across the face as hard as he could.

The man's head jerked to the side with the force of the blow and Billy Jack heard a wet snap as the man's neck broke; the man fell to the floor and didn't move anymore.

Turning back to his dad, Billy Jack started to panic. He reached down to grab a hold of his shirt while he tried to figure out what to do, only to realize he wasn't wearing one. His hands started to shake as he tried to process the situation. His dad wasn't moving and he didn't know what to do or who to tell.

"R. . .r. . .rest," he said, nodding his head. "Rest m. . .m. . .makes sick people b. . .b. . .better."

He picked up his dad's bloody body and took him into the master bedroom. He carefully laid him down on the bed and covered him with a blanket that was lying folded across the bottom.

Billy Jack knelt down on the floor beside the bed and held his dad's hand in his larger ones, occasionally reaching up to stroke his forehead.

"Y. . .y. . .you'll feel better s. . .s. . .soon, Dad," he whispered. "You j. . .j. . .just need rest."

In moments Billy Jack thought he saw results from the resting as Mr. Harper's eyes fluttered open and a low moan escaped his partially parted lips.

"Dad? Y. . .y. . .you feel better?" Billy Jack asked, standing. "C. . .c. . .can I get you anything?"

Mr. Harper didn't answer, he just groaned and turned his cloudy eyes toward Billy Jack and that's when he knew something wasn't right; the man who'd attacked his dad had eyes like that.

Clawing viciously at the blanket, trying to get free, Mr. Harper's jaw snapped open and shut, clicking loudly.

"Dad?" Billy Jack asked in a voice that could have passed for a child's. "What's w. . .w. . .wrong with y. . .y. . .you?"

His dad didn't answer, but broke free of the blanket to stand. Blood gushed from his open stomach, carrying his intestines with it. They splashed onto the scuffed, hardwood floor with a *squish.* He stepped forward, into his own mess, slipping slightly, but righting himself again with the help of the bed, and advanced toward Billy Jack sniffing loudly and moaning.

Billy Jack backed away and bumped against a stand that a TV was sitting on, knocking the TV off; the screen shattered on the floor. He became more flustered and tried to pick up the TV and put it back.

"I'm s. . .s. . .sorry, Dad," he gushed. "I d. . .d. . .didn't mean to b. . .b. . .break your TV."

Mr. Harper's hand fell heavily on Billy Jack's shoulder, and he stood and turned to face his father, who hissed menacingly in his face. He lunged at Billy Jack trying to bite him.

Billy Jack screamed and fell backwards as he instinctively dodged the bite, falling into the glass; it cut into his back and side, but he didn't notice as his fear was focused on his sick parent.

"Why are y. . .y. . .you trying to e. . .e. . .eat me?" he whimpered, sitting up slightly and scooting backwards on his butt.

Mr. Harper roared and lunged at Billy Jack, who brought his arms up to defend himself, knocking his dad hard in the chin and off of him. Frantically, he grabbed at things around him as his dad pounced him once more. He lifted a large piece of glass and shoved it upward. It went in through the bottom of his dad's chin at an angle, sinking deep into his head and brain.

Mr. Harper went still with a gurgle.

Billy Jack shoved his dad's body off of himself and took deep, sobbing breaths. He didn't understand why his dad had tried to bite him. He'd thought his dad loved him, but now he wasn't so sure.

Sitting up, he looked around the room, noticing that he'd knocked the door of the TV stand open when he'd bumped into it. Some misplaced impulse made it impossible for him not to fix it; normally he would get in trouble for not closing doors. Rising up on his knees, he crawled through the glass toward it, noting for the first time that he was hurt. As his hand met the dark, painted wood, he eyes caught sight of something bright and colorful inside. Frowning, he opened the door further to find his comic books stacked inside. A grin spread across his blood spattered face. *Dad did love me*, he thought, glancing at the dead body on the floor to his right with an ache in his heart. All he'd ever heard from his father were mean things: how dumb he was; how Billy Jack's mother had left because she couldn't handle living with a child like him; how hard his life was trying to provide for him and meet his "special" needs; and how he couldn't have a life because what woman would want anything to do with the father of a big dummy like him. But deep down, in spite of everything, his dad really, truly had loved him, and to Billy Jack, the comic books proved it.

"Daddy," Billy Jack whimpered and turned, lifting his dad's body into his arms, hugging it tight, weeping. "I l. . .l. . .love you." He cried and rocked his dad's body for a long time, before he laid the body back onto the bed.

He went down the hall and into the bathroom and was about to use the toilet when he noticed how filthy he was; he was completely covered in blood. Freaking out slightly, he stripped off his clothes as fast as he could and climbed into the shower, screaming as the water hit his wounds when he turned it on. He pulled out all the shards of glass that he could, but he couldn't reach them all. They didn't really hurt unless the water hit them directly, so he didn't worry about them. After cleaning himself, he stepped out of the shower and toweled dry, realizing for the first time he didn't have any clothes to put on and he'd have to go to his room to get some.

Cautiously, he opened the bathroom door, half-expecting another scary person to jump out of nowhere and try to bite him, but the apartment was silent. Just as he was stepping out into the hall the sound of static behind him made him jump and cry out, clutching his chest in fear.

"Billy Jack?" came a faint, young voice from his bloody pants.

He walked slowly over to them and stared down at them, frowning. *Why are my pants talking?* he wondered. The voice spoke again, making him jump back in surprise.

"Billy Jack? It's Mike. I'm scared. Mommy is acting funny and is trying to bite me. Help!"

"The w. . .w. . .walkie-talkie!" Billy Jack exclaimed. He reached forward and picked up his pants, frantically searching them until he found the toy he'd mistakenly taken from his friend's house. Pressing the button he spoke into it, "Mike! I'll c. . .c. . .come rescue y. . .y. . .you!"

"Hurry!" Mike's little voice cried.

"I'm c. . .c. . .coming!" Billy Jack screamed into the speaker on the plastic box, shaking it hard when he didn't get a response. "Oh, n. . .n. . .no! I c. . .c. . .can't hear you anymore, Mike!" He turned knobs, pressed the button and shook the walkie-talkie, but didn't get a response.

No longer caring that he was naked, or that he was bloody again from handling his pants, Billy Jack darted through the apartment and into his bedroom. Without hesitation he put on the superhero uniform he'd made, and in his mind he became Super Billy Jack, savior of all who lived in the cursed castle! He would save his little friend and save the day!

First he put on his red flannel union suit with the lightning bolt and the letters B and J on the chest. Next he slipped on the bright green galoshes he'd bought with his allowance money. Lastly, he put on his hat. It was a multicolored beanie with a little propeller on top that would keep the cursed castle keepers from reading his thoughts; he'd attached a strip of material with holes where his eyes were, to the front, to hang down over his face and protect his identity.

Proudly he stood admiring himself in the mirror for a moment with his feet wide apart and his fists on his hips.

"Super Billy Jack t. . .t. . .to the rescue!" he yelled, and dashed out of his bedroom.

He paused for a moment at the door of the apartment, remembering his dad said that he shouldn't go out dressed like he was or he would take his comic books. But he knew his dad wasn't coming back this time and that he wouldn't take his comic books again, so with a grin, he charged out into the hall. He was disappointed when nothing was going on in the hall, but quickly lifted his spirits by pretending to fly to the elevator. Echoing the ding when the door opened, he hopped inside and spun in a full circling saying, "Whaaaa!" before he pushed the button that would take him to the lobby.

When the door slid open, he ran out into the lobby to witness one of the buildings tenants being attacked by a group of three biting men. Her screams grew weaker and weaker as blood sprayed into the air from her neck where a large patch of skin was missing and an artery had been ruptured. The blood landed on his bright green boots and ran down the side to pool around his feet as he stood in shock before he took action.

Screaming, he darted across the hall, bravely facing the mailbox monster to attack the men consuming the woman. He slammed his fist into the back of one of the men's heads and his fist sank into the man's skull. He shook it off in disgust, drawing the attention of the other two men as he did so. They shuffled away from the woman, allowing her dead, bloody, limp body to fall to the floor, hissing at him.

Their eyes were cloudy and parts of their faces were missing. They walked awkwardly and drooled blood out of their wide-open mouths.

"You c. . .c. . .cursed creatures won't g. . .g. . .get the best of m. . .m. . .me!" Billy Jack shouted, and reached out and grabbing both of the men's heads, slamming them together. They burst like two overly ripe melons under the pressure of the collision; chunks of brain and clotted, black blood flew in every direction.

He pulled his hands away and let the bodies drop to the floor.

"Ew," he said looking down at the pile of bodies in front of him and at the mess they'd made. "I sh. . .sh. . .should clean this m. . .m. . .mess up, but I h. . .h. . .have to save Mike!"

Turning, he darted toward the door to the stairwell, but slipped in pooled blood and fell back onto the pile of death.

He screamed and kicked, trying to fight his way out of the slop. Finally rolling off, he crawled to the door to the stairs, breathing heavily. *Being a superhero is harder than I thought it would be,* he thought, holding onto the door handle while he regained his footing. Pulling open the door, he headed into the darkness and almost felt like he was being swallowed whole by the building itself, so he started singing the song that always gave him courage when he had to do big things that scared him: Itsy-Bitsy-Spider.

With his whispering voice echoing off the stark walls, Billy Jack climbed the stairs as fast as he could, slipping occasionally because the blood dripping from his clothes and onto the worn-smooth stairs made them slicker than normal.

As he reached the fourth floor landing, he heard a low moan echo around him. He froze, not knowing what to do, but knowing someone else was close-by. He felt along the wall for the door leading to the fourth floor hallway, and looked through the gloom created by the wane moonlight seeping in through the small, dirty, barred windows high in the walls. His hand reached the handle as he heard a louder moan and a *thump*ing noise of something falling down stairs and a deep groan; it sounded closer. He raised his eyes to the fifth floor landing as his hand gripped the door handle tighter; something was moving around up there, groaning. It had to be another of the biting people.

The form slowly stood and limped to the edge of the landing, looking down at Billy Jack. It groaned loudly and tried to walk forward, falling down the stairs right at him.

Billy Jack screamed, yanked the door open, and darted onto the fourth floor of the building. Making sure the door was shut tight behind him, he spun and darted, not paying attention to anything around him. He slammed into a woman and pinned her against the wall with all of his weight.

She gasped and then purred, "Hold on, sugar, and I'll give you anything you want." Her hand – which was caught between them – cupped his crotch.

Billy Jack cried out and backed away. "Why d. . .d. . .did you touch me th. . .th. . .there?" he whimpered, holding his hands over his penis like he had to pee.

The woman laughed and advanced toward him, looking him over. "You pay me enough I'll give you what you really want." She traced the B and J on his chest with her finger. "You like BJs, don't you?" she teased, and then frowned. "Why are you all wet?"

Holding her hand up at an angle to the faint hallway light, she saw that her hand was covered with blood; she looked down and discovered that her body was also coated in blood where his had touched hers when he'd pinned her to the wall.

"It's blood!" she screamed, and darted for the stairwell door.

Billy Jack yelled, "No!" and tried to stop her from opening the door, but it was too late.

"Holy shit, a zombie!" she yelped, and tried turning back to Billy Jack, who was standing, panting, in the hall.

He glimpsed the stark fear in her eyes as the man she'd identified as a zombie fell on her from behind, pinning her to the floor. She screamed and kicked, but it was too late, the monster's teeth had sunk into her flesh and she was bleeding.

Billy Jack was scared, still standing in the hall, cupping his privates, in shock over what had happened so quickly. He knew he needed to get back out into the stairwell to keep climbing and save Mike. To reach the stairs he would have to go through the zombie attacking the strange, almost naked, woman who liked to touch people in their no-no-special places.

Tugging at the front of his union suit, he decided he would have to stop the zombie from hurting the woman, or else he wouldn't be a real superhero – they saved everyone.

With a roar, he charged forward, getting the zombie's attention; it lifted its head at the noise. Hopping slightly, he planted one foot hard on the floor and kicked with the other like he'd seen football players do on TV when they were kicking a field goal. His kicking foot connected with the zombie's chin, snapping its head back and almost off as its rotting flesh tore.

The woman was still alive and sobbing uncontrollably, so Billy Jack dragged the zombie off of the woman and helped her up. She was weak and wobbled back and forth.

"You n. . .n. . .need to rest, m. . .m. . .ma'am," he said, leaning her up against the wall; she slid down, sitting hard on her butt when he let her go. "I h. . .h. . .have to save Mike."

Billy Jack opened the door to the stairwell a little further – the zombie's legs were holding it open slightly – and he disappeared into the oppressive gloom once again. He was now scared that there would be more of the zombie creatures on the stairs somewhere waiting to get him, so he ran up the five flights of stairs to the ninth floor. Ripping open the door, he carefully stepped into the hallway and looked around before closing the door behind himself.

The hall was silent; there was no sound of anyone anywhere, not even noise from TVs in the apartments. The moon cast shadows along the corridor and made Billy Jack more and more nervous. He tugged at the front of his union suit, accidentally popping off a button, but he didn't notice. He was focused on the scary world around him, gulping and whimpering in succession. The idea of being a superhero had been fun when the world was safe and he was only dealing with his imagination, but it was more difficult than he'd anticipated, and more scary. He finally reached apartment 947 and what he found didn't improve his spirits any.

A smeared, bloody hand print was bright on the wide-open door. From within the apartment he heard growling and the wet sound of something eating, along with soft whimpers. Tentatively, he stepped over the threshold and beheld a gruesome sight on the kitchen floor.

Mike's bare feet were twitching and bouncing off the floor as his mother and some man Billy Jack didn't know – both naked – ate his small body. The whimpers were Mike's and Billy Jack realized he was still alive. Rage and grief surged through him and he screamed at the zombies.

"S. . .s. . .stop hurting my f. . .f. . .friend!"

He stormed into the room and grabbed the man, wrapping his hands around his neck, squeezing with all his strength. The man hadn't been a zombie long, so he wasn't rotting, but when Billy Jack gave him a quick jerk in his fury, his spine snapped just below his skull and he went still. Throwing the limp body off to the side, Billy Jack kicked Mike's mom in the head; she had been too interested in eating her son to pay attention to what was going on around her. He picked her up by the shoulders and slammed her against the wall screaming at her for being a bad mother, until her skull cracked and a wet slapping sound rang through the kitchen each time she hit the wall. With tears running down his cheeks, Billy Jack let her fall to the floor as well, and turned to kneel down beside Mike.

His little body was quivering as he took each breath. Blood was oozing from his body and soaking into the scraps of what used to be his clothes. "Billy Jack," he whispered, "thank you for saving me."

Billy Jack was too choked up with tears to respond and slid his arm under his small friend's head, hugging him close, rocking gently.

After a couple more shaky intakes of air, Mike stopped breathing altogether. Billy Jack continued to rock him, wailing, mourning his friend more than he'd mourned his father; they'd been closer and had a real bond.

He was too caught up in his grief to notice that all the noise he was making had attracted more zombies. Three of them came shambling through the door and were clawing at him before he knew what was going on. In his grief he batted their clawing hands away, but only half-heartedly. With Mike gone he didn't care what happened to him. He snapped back to reality when the small body moved in his arms, moaning insistently. Sudden sharp pains from his neck, chest, and arm caused him to cry out and stand. He jumped back and dropped Mike on the blood-soaked floor; his once angelic face was twisted in blood lust.

"Mike?" Billy Jack stammered, barely noticing that the small boy had bitten him, as had two others of the undead ranks. "A. . .a. . .are you okay?"

Mike hissed and tried to stand, but the damage to his body had been too extensive; the middle of his body was gone, all the way to his spinal cord. With a harsh grunt, the zombie boy flipped himself over onto his front and flopped like a fish toward Billy Jack, licking what little blood he'd drawn from his tiny lips.

"N. . .n. . .no!" Billy Jack sobbed, backing away.

One of the other zombies had finally had enough of everything and lunged at Billy Jack. He jumped and dodged the sudden movement, only to slip in the huge puddle of blood on the floor and fall hard. All three of the adult zombies piled onto him, tearing skin and muscle with their teeth and devouring sweet, hot flesh, but Billy Jack didn't even cry out with pain. His eyes were locked with the now cloudy eyes of Mike as he flopped closer and closer. He was crying and was slipping into shock, seeing his once best friend turn into a blood thirsty creature was just too much.

By the time Mike finally reached Billy Jack, he was weak from loss of blood, but the zombie didn't care because it worked to his advantage. He growl/purred down at his meal like the man was a steak and not a friend.

"I'm s. . .s. . .sorry, Mike," Billy Jack whispered. "I'm s. . .s. . .sorry I didn't m. . .m. . .make it here in t. . .t. . .time. I'm sorry I c. . .c. . .couldn't be your s. . .s. . .superhero. I g. . .g. . .guess I'm a w. . .w. . .worthless nothing l. . .l. . .like my dad s. . .s. . .said. . ."

Mike's mouth closed around Billy Jack's throat, cutting off his air. Pulling back, he tore off a small chunk of flesh, but his small teeth had done the job. They'd found an artery, and soon Billy Jack wasn't suffering any longer and the zombies drank their fill of his bloody, until he too rose again to feast on the living.

HISTORICAL SIGNIFICANCE

Perry Roberts stood at the top of the stairs, staring down into the black depths of his basement. He held the last box that needed to be stored down there, but he couldn't make his legs move. *The light was on when I went outside, wasn't it?* he thought. He knew it had been, but now it was out.

With a sigh, he sat the box down on the floor, reached into the slight gloom at the top of the stairwell, and felt the switch with his fingers; it was still on. *Bulb must've blown*, he thought to himself with another, deeper sigh.

Thinking hard, he remembered unpacking a box with spare bulbs earlier and headed to the laundry room to retrieved one, also grabbing the flashlight he'd stored there. Grumbling under his breath, he descended into the dark depths of his basement. It smelled musty, damp, and slightly metallic; the air noticeably dropped in temperature with each step. The house was old, having been one of the first built in the small New England town, and the basement was designed to hold the cold so that home-canned goods and other food necessities could be stored there.

"Lots of history," the real-estate agent had said. "Not many places like this left for just anyone to buy."

Being the history buff that he was, he couldn't help but be drawn to its charm, even though it had sat empty for more than a decade and had to be drastically updated before he could move in. One of the things he'd found most fascinating about the place was the old player piano sitting in the corner of the basement. He couldn't figure out how it had gotten down there – the stairs were too narrow and the basement walls consisted of large, rectangle slabs of limestone that looked like they'd been there for hundreds of years.

With the help of his flashlight, he removed the old bulb and shook it beside his ear, and sure enough, he heard the filament rattle. Tucking the flashlight under his chin so he could use both hands, he slid the burned out bulb into the front pouch of his hoodie and extracted the other. As he screwed in the new bulb he forgot the switch was still on and didn't close his eyes. When the bright glow of the 75 watt bulb flared to life, he dropped the flashlight with a loud *clang* and squeezed his eyes tightly shut. After a moment, he started blinking rapidly and looking around the room. Bodies in old fashion clothing lay everywhere – some holding bottles of whiskey or tankards of ale. Slowly they sat up and then stood with leering grins, looking him over like he was a succulent piece of meat. They advanced toward him and Perry spun around; he was completely surrounded and the closer they came the more the temperature of the air around him dropped. He tried to focus on them directly, but the light spots in his eyes prevented him from doing so; as his vision cleared the images began to disappear. Almost in a panic, thinking he was being attacked, he spun around in a circle with his arms up defensively, looking for assailants. None were there. All he could see now were the leaning shadows cast by the stairs and the stacked boxes; the rough, bare rock of the walls and floor echoed his harsh breathing back to him, giving him a chill that had nothing to do with the climate of the room.

After dropping his arms, taking a couple of deep breaths, and doing another thorough visual examination of the entire room, he shrugged the occurrence off as his imagination. He bent down and picked up the pieces of his flashlight – having broken it when he dropped it on the hard floor – before he went upstairs, dumped the ruined flashlight in the trash, and carried down the last box. But he couldn't shake the feeling that someone was down in the basement with him, and he kept looking over his shoulder expecting to find them standing behind him, ready to hurt him. He was beginning to wonder if the house might be haunted, but then reminded himself he didn't believe in ghosts.

With an effort he forced himself to calm down, and after stacking the box with the others he had in the corner, he headed toward the stairs. Pausing, he glanced around one more time and ran his fingers over the now yellow keys of the player piano, wondering if he could get the old thing working. Once again he pondered on how the piano had come to be in the basement and couldn't come up with a reasonable explanation.

"Maybe the ghosts brought it downstairs," he said with a mocking laugh.

As soon as the words left his mouth a chill ran down his spine and the hairs on the back of his neck stood on end as the air around him suddenly dropped in temperature and he felt like he was being stalked again. Not needing any more encouragement, he jogged up the stairs and could have sworn he'd heard a deep, masculine laugh echo from behind him.

Back upstairs, he turned off the basement light and slammed the short, rough plank door behind him, making sure the old, wrought-iron latch was secure. He pressed both his hands on the door and leaned against it, taking deep, calming breaths, feeling silly about his reaction to his imagination running wild.

"There's no such thing as ghosts . . . There's no such thing as ghosts . . ." he repeated to himself over and over again, as if in saying it he could dispel the horrible feelings he'd had downstairs.

Perry heard a knock at his front door and almost jumped out of his skin at the sudden and unexpected noise; he stepped from the kitchen into the short, narrow hallway and spied his friend John through the door's window.

"Hold on!" he yelled, rushing forward and letting his friend in, glad for the distraction. "What's up?"

John grinned. "Five days 'til Halloween! What do you think's up? We need costumes and a lot of ghoulish stuff to decorate this spooky old house of yours."

Perry laughed and all of his trepidation melted away as he focused on his friend and pushed everything else from his mind. "How could I forget?"

John smacked his forehead in a "Duh!" gesture and pointed with his thumb to his Chevy pickup parked at the curb. "I'll be out there. Hurry up!"

With that John turned and practically hopped down the limestone block porch steps. He hadn't been too happy when Perry had decided to move here, wishing his friend would stay closer, but he'd handled it well. They'd known each other all their lives and had just recently graduated from separate colleges. Over the past summer they'd spent a lot of time together catching up, and now they were separated again; growing up was indeed hard to do.

Donning a light jacket over his hoodie – taken from a hook by the door – Perry stepped out into the brisk October wind. Red, gold, and brown leaves littered the yard and street, leaving behind dark skeleton trees to moan eerily as their bare branches danced in the wind. He pushed his hands into the front pouch of his hoodie and his hands came in contact with the light bulb he'd removed downstairs and, for a moment, the memories of his experiences returned. He tossed it in the large trash can sitting in the corner of his enclosed porch, as if ridding himself of the bulb also discarded the disturbing memories permanently, and hurried to join John.

~ * ~

Their day went fast. They'd each found a costume they loved: John, a ghoul of disgusting proportions; and Perry, a very bloody looking zombie. They'd also picked up an array of fake tomb stones and bones to litter in Perry's yard, to serve as decorations for the huge Halloween party they were planning.

"Stop by the library, would ya?" Perry asked on their way back to his house. "I had the librarian look up some historical information on my house and I need to pick it up." He paused for a moment and almost continued, asking John if he believed in ghosts, but with a shake of his head he decided not to waste any more time on nonsense.

John raised his eyebrows at Perry's undecided movements, but when he didn't say anything more, he nodded consent and drove to the small, out-of-the-way library that served the town.

It took Perry less than ten minutes to retrieve the information he'd requested. John laughed hysterically as he watched his friend come stumbling out of the local library, weighed down with books and printouts of old newspapers.

"Are you writing a book series?" John teased as he leaned over and pushed open the truck door for Perry. "Looks like you have enough research there for five!"

Scowling, Perry managed to maneuver himself, and his load, into the truck. "I didn't know they'd find this much. Now I feel like I'm back in school!"

John laughed again, shook his head, and drove them back to Perry's place. They unloaded all their Halloween goodies and discussed the party briefly before John left; he had work early the next day and he knew Perry was itching to get at the materials he'd picked up from the library.

For the next few days Perry poured over the books and old newspaper articles, learning about his new house and its history. He wanted to get through as much of it as possible before the party, and before he had to start his new job; he would begin his career as a website designer the second week of November. The information the librarian had gleaned was very interesting. Apparently the house he was living in used to be a small time, bar-like establishment. It was known for its many visitors of "questionable virtue" and after reading some of the articles, he knew that meant men who lived outside the law. A couple of people had even been murdered in the house, which made him again think of the occurrences in the basement.

One picture particularly interested him. It was taken on October 31st of 1872, according to the notation under the photo. The player piano was in it, but the photograph had been taken in his living room. The people in the photo looked like the ones he'd thought he'd seen in the basement, but he couldn't be sure because most of them were wearing festive masks depicting demons. The clothing style was the same, as were the bottles and tankards, but he figured what happened could still have been just his imagination. After all, he'd seen plenty of the same in old movies.

The article beneath the picture spoke briefly about the Halloween party, and how wild they'd gotten, referring to a couple of rough men who were believed to have been associated with the occult. As he read on, he was disappointed to find that most of the article was missing due to the photocopier running out of toner, at least that's what he ascertained from the spotty black ink on the rest of the page. With a crocked grin, he looked back at the photo, thinking it would be great to show it to John, since they too were having a Halloween party in the house. As he laid the paper aside, he didn't notice the date on the top – for the article – was for November

1st, 1872, or that the rest of the article was printed clearly on the back telling of the horrible events of the night of that party, and how no one who'd attended had ever been seen again.

~ * ~

On the night of October 30th, Perry lay down in bed, excited about the party that would take place the following evening. Thoughts swirled through his head about all that needed to be done, and about a certain woman he'd invited, hoping she'd attend. Even with these thoughts it didn't take his exhausted body long to fall asleep.

Shortly after midnight, icy hands gripped Perry's ankles and fingernails penetrated his flesh like icicles, startling him out of his warm cocoon of sleep. He cried out and struggled, feeling hot, slick, wet blood seep from his wounds and soak into his bed, but his efforts didn't deter the grip that was dragging him out of bed with astounding force and strength. He screamed and grabbed at the sheets, blankets, and mattress, trying to save himself, to no avail.

He hit the floor with a hard, resounding *smack*. His head bounced off the hardwood with a loud *thud* that almost knocked him unconscious; blood gushed out of a gash on his head from where it had hit the metal bedframe during the struggle, falling into his eyes, and making the floor slick. Blinking rapidly, he tried to stay awake and twisted around to get a glimpse of who was assaulting him. He yelled, telling whoever it was to stop, and asking why they were doing it.

The darkness prevented him from seeing anyone or anything, and the more he struggled the tighter the grip on his ankles became; he heard his bones crack and felt the shards of their splinters escaping the encasement of his flesh. Crying out from the pain, and imagining that his ankles now looked like pin cushions because of the protruding bones,

Perry tried to grab onto anything he could, but it was no use. Every time he would get a grip on something his attacker would either yank him so hard that eventually his fingers broke with loud pops or he would be lifted slightly into the air and slammed back down onto the floor until he let go.

The violence continued as he was dragged down the stairs, and Perry suffered so much head trauma that by the time he was on the first floor the world around him was nothing more than a blur seen through drops of blood, flowing from multiple gashes all over his bruised head. And as he was dragged toward the kitchen – where he left a light on all night – he saw that no one and nothing was there; he was being attacked by an invisible force and thought for the first time that he might have been wrong about ghosts.

He heard the piano playing downstairs and laughter with it. *What's going on?* he thought before he was finally knocked completely unconscious by a battering from the basement stairs.

~ * ~

Perry regained awareness slowly. He was lying on the cold basement floor in nothing but his boxer shorts. He shivered and tried to curl into a ball to conserve his body heat. A harsh male laugh barked behind him, making him jump. Turning his head sharply, he beheld a group of seven men and two women. They were all dressed in clothes from the 1800s. He blinked and frowned. His head hurt beyond belief and his hips, legs, and ankles throbbed. Weak and disoriented, he couldn't focus or speak.

Desperation soon overcame his weakness when he saw them moving toward him. They didn't have legs, but floated a foot and a half above the stone floor. The closer they got to him the more transparent they became. Frantically, he tried to crawl toward the stairs, hissing and whimpering at the pain in his ankles and head, but didn't make it. Cold seeped into his body, causing him to shiver more violently, as the "spirits" came closer, surrounding him and laughing.

"Sweet hot blood . . . " one of the men said.

" . . . and meat!" one of the women exclaimed, and cackled.

"What should we do with him?" another one of the men asked.

"Let's eat him," the first man said again.

"Wasn't he going to have a party tonight?" another feminine voice said almost coyly. "Maybe we should possess him and have our fill of the guests!"

The group laughed and jeered in agreement; many to feast upon was better than one.

One by one the spirits drifted over Perry and sank into his body. He screamed as his body temperature dropped and he felt his consciousness being forced deeper and deeper inside himself. He knew no one would hear him but he still called out for help. Even if he had been lucky and someone did come to his aid, he knew there was nothing anyone could do.

"He's damaged!" one of the women said inside him. "Someone will notice!"

"She's right, you know," said the other feminine voice. "We'll have to clean him up."

"I've got it," one of the men said with a laugh. "I'll have him fixed up momentarily!"

Perry convulsed in excruciating pain as his frigid body popped and snapped, healing itself of the wounds which had been inflicted upon him during the attack.

"Lovely," the first female voice sighed.

"Please stop," Perry cried out from the box inside himself he'd been pressed into; his consciousness was pushed back and he had no control over his body, but he could still feel everything that happened to his physical self. "Kill me, but don't torture me like this . . . Please!"

"Oh, shut up!" one of the men yelled, and the rest of the unwelcome spirits inhabiting Perry's body laughed.

"What should we do with him until the party?" one of the male voices asked.

"He's still all bloody . . . Why don't we give him a bath?" asked one of the female voices.

"Oh, yes," said the other female voice with a giggle.

"You ladies have your fun, but I want no part of it," a male voice said with slight amusement and a bit of disgust.

The females giggled again and Perry felt himself rising up to a standing position. Awkwardly his body ascended the stairs and he noted that he could see everything around him, but still had no say or control over his body.

Before he was ready, they were in the bathroom and his shorts were being removed.

"My, my, what do we have here?" one of the female voices asked snidely. "Seems we have a naked man to play with."

"Share!" the other female voice yelled. "You get one hand and I get the other."

Perry could feel the women becoming more prominent in his body and the male entities slipped back and almost felt like they were sleeping.

"All right, all right," the first female voice said. "I'll share."

They both giggled as they shut the door to the bathroom and found a full length mirror hanging on the door.

"Oh, what fun!" the second female voice squealed.

"Yes, indeed," the other said with smug satisfaction.

Soon Perry's hands were traveling all over his body, doing things to himself against his will.

"Please stop!" he groaned from deep within as he was forced to watch and feel what the female spirits were doing to him.

"Don't you like it, luv?" one voice asked, and both the females laughed.

"Stop!" he screamed, but they just continued to laugh at him.

It took over an hour for them to play games with him and molest him in the shower, after which he felt more dirty than clean; they'd done unimaginable things to his body.

~ * ~

Later that day, John arrived to help with the Halloween party, letting himself in with the key Perry had given him when there was no response to his knock. As he turned from shutting the door, he spotted Perry standing silently at the top of the stairway in his zombie costume.

"Hey, man," John said, as he jumped in startled surprise. "You scared the crap out of me!" He looked his friend over and grinned. "You're costume is intense, but I thought we weren't going to change until after we had things set up for the party."

Perry's body just stood there with its eyes staring down at John while the spirits inside argued about how to answer the question and handle this newcomer; they finally came to a decision.

"Hello, Earth to Perry," John said, looking slightly worried and confused at the foot of the stairs. "You okay, man?"

"I'm fine," Perry's voice said, being controlled by one of the males. "I was excited and decided to don my festive apparel early."

"You sound strange," John said, his confused frown deepening. "What's with all the 'don my festive apparel' shit? You sound old or something."

Perry's face sneered at John behind the zombie make-up as he descended the stairs toward him. When he reached the bottom step his arm shot out and he wrapped his hand around John's throat, squeezing and lifting him off his feet.

"You're a cheeky bloke," a strange masculine voice said, using Perry's mouth, no longer trying to disguise himself. "I don't like being called old!"

John dropped the bags of stuff he was carrying and tried to pry the strong hand from his throat so he could breathe; he kicked and clawed at Perry's hand and arm as he was lifted off the floor.

"Now we have to do something with him," Perry heard one of the male voices say as they again began talking internally to each other.

"It is crowded in here," another said, "maybe some of us should possess him, so we'll have more space to move around and breathe!"

The other voices agreed and started to argue about who would go and who would stay. Perry broke into their argument . . .

"If you are going to do something, do it soon!" he yelled. "Otherwise you'll kill my friend and have nowhere to go!"

The voices quieted for a moment and Perry's hand loosened slightly on John's throat, allowing him strained breathing rather than none at all.

"I think Ginger, Frank, Paul, and Peter should go," one of the female voices said.

It was the first time Perry had heard them refer to each other by name and listened carefully. Something about the names seemed familiar, but he couldn't place them. Then it hit him! Those were some of the names of the people who'd attended the Halloween party in the old newspaper article! He wished now, more than ever, that he'd been able to read the end of the article, so he could know what had happened, and was going to happen.

They argued some more and then Perry felt his small containment area expand. Four of the spirits drifted out of his body and into John's, who was instantly released. He fell gasping to the floor and started thrashing around, screaming, and clutching at his body. Finally, he stilled and looked around with eyes that weren't his own.

Perry cringed and whispered, "Sorry, my friend." He wished John hadn't gotten involved, and more than anything he wished he would have mentioned what had happened in the basement a few days before, thinking this wouldn't have happened if he'd acknowledged it. He also thought about the horrible experience he'd had earlier in the bathroom and hoped his friend wouldn't have to endure something similar when he changed into his costume; as if reading his thoughts, the female spirit who was still inside him laughed softly.

"He might like it, luv," she said. "After all, you seemed to enjoy some of it." She cackled with a perverse laugh and Perry didn't respond.

~ * ~

It didn't take the spirits long to master the control they had over Perry and John, and they extracted from their brains and thoughts all the things that needed to be done to prepare for the party; they'd just finished when the first guest arrived.

Nicole Winters – the tall, raven-haired, blue-eyed beauty who lived just down the street – stood on the porch with her coat hanging slightly open. Perry heart sank when he was forced to open the door and let her in. She smiled broadly, sporting a sexy fairy costume that would have made him drool if he hadn't been possessed by crazy entities from the past; some of the comments the male ones were making about her made him panic and try to take back control.

"Run, Nicole!" Perry screamed. "Run!"

But of course, she couldn't hear him, he still couldn't control any part of his body, including his vocal cords.

"Shut up, you," one of the males growled. "We'll have our fun with this little tart and there's nothing you can do about it."

"Thanks for inviting me, Perry," Nicole said, stepping inside and sliding off her coat, revealing more of her costume, or lack thereof. Most of it was sheer and see through; the male spirits were going wild.

"Ever seen any dressin's like 'em fellas?" one of them asked.

"No, but I'd like to tear them off with my teeth and devour what's underneath!" another exclaimed.

John entered the hallway, coming from the kitchen, and Perry saw a reflection in his eyes of what he was hearing within.

"I'm glad you could make it," Perry's pleasant voice said, as his hand was placed on her butt and he squeezed.

Nicole gasped and giggled, giving him a wink. "I wouldn't have missed it. I love Halloween parties. They give me an excuse to dress up." She was pressing herself against his body now and practically purring with wicked intent in her eyes.

"Oh, yeah, boys," one of the voices said. "We're gonna have us a slice of that Heaven."

They all laughed.

Perry cringed and wished there was something he could do to stop all this, but he couldn't think of anything.

John walked down the hall toward them and pressed up against Nicole from the back, trapping her between them. He bent forward and whispered something in her ear that Perry didn't catch. He knew it wasn't John doing any of it, but he still felt betrayed for some strange reason.

Nicole jerked and struggled, trying to break free, just before her personality flipped and she giggled and sighed, accepting the attention from both men. Perry and John realized instantly when their containment expanded slightly that the female spirits had both moved into Nicole's body. She began to wiggle against and grope both of the men, and pouted when someone knocked on the front door.

"Bloody hell!" she growled. "All these interruptions are spoiling our fun!"

Both of the possessed men laughed. None of them were themselves any longer and just watched and felt everything that happened around them.

Guests continued to arrive for the next forty-five minutes and none of them knew a thing about what was going on. If Nicole, John, or Perry did something strange, the guests would just shrug it off, assuming they'd already started drinking.

A couple times Nicole disappeared from the room with John, and a couple of times she left with Perry. No one really noticed, but Perry was devastated; he really liked and cared for Nicole, and the damned possessing spirits were making them both do tainted and lewd things to each other. He didn't even want to think about what she was doing with John, knowing it was probably just as bad or worse.

"Why are you doing this to us?" Perry asked as he was again entering the living room where the party was, after being with Nicole. "Why not just kill us? Why play with us like this first?"

"Well, you see . . . " one of the voices started in a teasing manner.

"Don't tell 'im!" another barked. "Then he'll know!"

"What does it matter if he knows?" another asked. "He can't do anything about it."

"Just shut up, you," the second voice ordered. "It'll be over before you know it."

Everything kept moving smoothly along until around midnight, and then Perry's mouth announced that he wanted to show everyone the player piano in the basement. They were intrigued, so like cattle the twenty-three people at the party (including Perry, John, and Nicole) went down into the basement; Nicole was the last one and she shut the door tightly behind herself.

"What's going on?" Perry asked from deep within himself. "Why did you bring everyone down here?"

"Shut up!" all the voices barked at him.

Everyone was *oh*ing and *ah*ing over the piano while Perry, John, and Nicole stood at the base of the stairs. No one saw their eyes glow bright red, and no one saw the humans' bodies transform into red scaled monsters with vicious long claws and mouths full of long, sharp teeth. But they did hear the panting and growling that emanated from them; the guests all turned and screamed.

"It's been a long time since we've had human flesh," the once Nicole growled, running her long black tongue across her teeth. "I want the first bite."

Both the beings who were once John and Perry growled and stepped forward.

The crowd cringed and moved backwards, pressing themselves against the far wall.

The Nicole-demon lunged forward, and with one clamp down of her jaws, she ripped a woman's head clean off. Blood dripped from her mouth and onto the floor as she chewed the skull and slurped out the brains within before swallowing it all. The woman's body fell to the floor and her blood began to drain out onto the stones. Instantly a pentagram made of flames appeared on the floor, encompassing the entire room; the body burned and dissolved to nothing in the fire.

More and more bodies joined the first as limbs were torn from torsos and hips, devoured by the bodies that had earlier been possessed and were now transformed. They gorged themselves on the flesh of the frightened, screaming guests and didn't stop until they were all dead.

The three stood in the center of the pentagram panting. Their eyes were ablaze with adrenaline and their bodies were covered in the guts and blood they'd spilt.

"It's time for the last three," a deep, growling voice said from beneath them as the floor disappeared and turned into a raging, licking fire.

"Yes, master," the three growled.

The female spirits left the body of Nicole they'd inhabited, and instantly it turned back into human form with Nicole at the helm once again. She blinked in confusion and screamed as her body began to burn. Soon there was nothing left of her; the same happened to both of the men.

Once they were consumed the floor reappeared and the fire was gone. The spirits floated in the air, looking at each other.

"I guess that pays our debt to Hell for a few more years," one of the females said.

"Yes," a male said with a laugh. "Happy Halloween!"

~ * ~

Days passed and none of the cars in front of Perry's house moved. Neighbors became angry and then concerned. The police were called and they finally contacted Perry's family when they couldn't reach him.

A search ensued for Perry, John, and all of the others, to no avail.

When nothing and no one was found, Perry's house was emptied and sold.

No one noticed the newspaper article from long ago when it was thrown into the trash, and no one knew to be afraid of what lurked in the basement, waiting for the next Halloween.

MEMORIES

"Ya ever 'eard a rabbit scream?" The words came to Peter Martin's mind unbidden as the foggy night around him seemed to close in, almost suffocating him as the past slammed into his brain, trying to becoming the present.

He glanced in the rearview mirror and beheld the angelic, sleeping face of his one-year-old son. Then he looked to his side, where his beautiful wife was sleeping peacefully, facing away from him and toward the passenger side window. They were safe, calm, at peace, and this gave him a measured sense of ease. It didn't last long though, because the memories wouldn't rest. It was the kind of night they liked: cold, dark, and dismal. Pushing against the meager resistance of his brain, they came forth, and with them came the fear, the dread, and the pain . . .

~ * ~

"I love this song," Peter roared over the blasting radio, reaching up to crank the knob that would increase the volume even more.

Jordan laughed and started head banging in the passenger's seat, throwing his hands up with his fingers folded to make devil horns.

Peter grinned, took another long swig from his warm beer, and increased the pressure of his foot on the gas pedal. The car's engine roared with excited energy as it was fed more fuel, and the young boys continued to party as they sped through the fog filled night. The back road they were traveling on was curved and windy, but those facts didn't deter their increased speed; they cheered and hungered for more.

Suddenly, Peter lost control of the car as he attempted to take on a particularly sharp curve at over sixty miles per hour. The tires screeched loudly as they slid on the moist blacktop, and they careened off the road, spinning in a full circle, coming to a halt when the front, passenger's side fender met a large oak's trunk.

Drunk, high, and confused at the suddenness of the events, the boys sat dazed for a few moments, waiting for reality to process; it was slow in coming.

"Damn, man," Jordan said, "what the fuck just happened?"

Peter sat blinking for a moment with blood running down the side of his head from where it had hit, and shattered, the driver's side window.

"How the hell should I know?" he asked weakly.

Jordan couldn't see through the windshield, which was riddled with cracks, so he turned the hand crank attached to his door and peered out into the swirling fog; it cleared just enough for him to see the tree directly in front of him. The impact had driven the trunk almost halfway through the hood.

"Holy fuck!" he exclaimed. "Where the hell did that big bastard come from?"

Peter groaned. "Not so loud – my head hurts!"

"Sorry," Jordan muttered. "You gonna be okay? What the hell are we supposed to do now?"

"I think I'll live," Peter said, gently probing his head wound with his fingers. "Don't know, man . . . Walk?"

Jordan rolled his eyes and looked at Peter. "Thank you, captain-fucking-obvious! I don't think we could drive anywhere with a tree in the hood of the car."

Peter giggled and winced. "Did you get hurt at all?"

Jordan shook his head. "Nope."

"Lucky you," Peter said, and groaned.

"What do you say we get the hell out of here?" Jordan asked, trying to open his door, but found that he couldn't. "I don't want to get blown up in this hunk of metal if it explodes. Can you open your door?"

"It won't explode, ya ass!" Peter scolded. "The tree didn't hit the gas tank. Damn you're dumb sometimes." He tried his door; it opened easily. "There, ya feel better, jerk-off?"

"Oh, shut the fuck up and get out," Jordan barked, and started pushing Peter out of the car so he too could be free of the crumpled and crushed confines.

"Ass," Peter said again, and giggled, holding his head and trying to stay on his feet.

"Shut up," Jordan retorted, looking around them; the fog was thick and he couldn't see much. "Where the fuck are we?"

Peter shrugged and giggled again. "Don't know."

"Great!" Jordan yelled, throwing his arms in the air in a motion of frustration. The wreck had knocked him almost sober, since he hadn't smoked as much pot as Peter, who on the other hand, was still trashed. "Let's just find the fucking road and get the hell out of here."

Peter giggled again and started walking, heading further into the woods.

"No, dumb ass, this way," Jordan said, grabbing his arm and turning him toward the road – according to the skid marks from the tires in the dirt.

"Oopsies," Peter said. "Sorry."

In less than a minute their feet met the blacktop and they paused to consider the next leg of their journey.

"We'll go . . . " Jordan squinted, trying to see off into the distance, both ways, through the fog. "This way!"

With Jordan still holding onto Peter's arm, they set off down the road, walking on the blacktop so they wouldn't get more lost than they already were.

They stumbled through the darkness, jumping at each and every noise that drifted to them through the shroud of mist.

"What's that?" Peter asked, pointing off into the distance and almost falling as he tugged his arm free of Jordan's grasp.

"What's what?" Jordan snapped, grabbing a hold of Peter again when he almost tumbled off the other side of the road and into a stand of bushes. "I don't see anything."

Peter pulled his arm away again and took two shuffling steps forward. "That! It's a light."

Muttering and grumbling under his breath, Jordan stepped up behind his friend and squinted, not expecting to see anything. After a moment, a gap in the fog allowed them to glimpse what looked like a porch light in the far distance.

"Holy shit," Jordan said. "I think it's a house or something. Maybe they'll have a phone and we can call Mack to come get us . . . I'm not calling my dad, that's for sure."

Peter nodded solemnly but didn't say anything; he just started stumbling in the direction of the light.

Up ahead the blacktop curved sharply to the left and a small dirt driveway led off through the woods to the right, to what looked like a log cabin. They left the road and headed in the direction of the building. As they passed underneath a towering row of pine trees, the fog began to disperse and they could see the structure more clearly. In reality it was more of a leaning shack than a log cabin. Around the three, uneven block steps that led to the door of the shack, were all kinds of "treasures": a motor; a dented tin tub; tools; tractor tires; and many undistinguishable items.

"I hope they have a phone," Peter muttered, swaying as he stood at the base of the steps, looking around at the rusted old junk. "Looks like a place out of one of those old westerns or something . . . You think they have any Moon Shine?" He giggled with his hand over his mouth.

"If they don't have a phone, maybe they'll have something we can drive back to town or something," Jordan said, nudging Peter aside and stomping up the steps. He raised his hand to knock when the door suddenly flew open, outwardly. He stepped back with a yelp and twisted his ankle as his foot missed the majority of the next step down; he fell to the ground.

"What're ya'll doin' out 'ere makin' all that racket?" an old, stooped over man croaked angrily from the doorway; he shook from age and clung to the door frame for dear life.

"Do you have a phone?" Peter asked brazenly. "We had an accident a ways back and need to call a tow truck and a friend to come pick us up."

Jordan stood, wincing as he put pressure on his twisted ankle. The jar of the impact, when he'd fallen, made him realize he'd been injured in the wreck; his ribs hurt. The fall had also knocked the breath out of his body, and now his lungs burned as he tried desperately to acquire oxygen.

"Phone?" the old man screeched. "Yah, I gots a phone. Come on in 'ere and use it." He disappeared inside with a wave of his hand.

The boys glanced at each other, shrugged, and slowly followed. Stepping inside they were shocked to find out how small the shack was. The kitchen – nothing more than an old pot belly, cast iron stove and a bucket – was right inside the door. A bed, a table, and what looked to be a lounge area, were crammed into the rest of the room, which was no bigger than six feet by seven feet at best. The man was over in the far corner fiddling with an old rotary phone.

"'Ere ya go," the man said, stepping back and holding out the receiver.

Jordan limped forward and took the black object from the man, smiling weakly; he began to dial Mack's house.

"Why don't ya sit 'own and wipe 'at blood off yer face, young fella?" the man said to Peter, tossing him a wet rag and motioning to the table. "Ya 'ungry?"

"Sure," Peter said, sitting down and dabbing at his wound. "I could eat a little something. What do you have?"

"Rabbit stew," the man said, walking over to the stove and lifting the lid off a pot sitting close to the back; the aroma of the stew drifted to Peter, making his stomach growl.

"That sure does smell good," Peter said. "Where did you get the rabbit to make rabbit stew?"

"Butchered it meself," the man said. "Ya ever 'eard a rabbit scream?"

Blinking blankly, Peter stared at the old man, a little bothered by the turn of the conversation.

The old man smirked. "Sounds like a pig squealin' off in 'e distance, crossed with 'e sound of nails on one o' 'em chalk boards. 'N eerie sound, it is."

Jordan, having hung up the phone, put his hand on Peter's shoulder and was about to say something to him when he caught what the man was saying; it shocked him into silence.

"This 'un was a fighter, 'e was. Screamin' 'e 'ole time. I clobbered 'im in 'e 'ead, but still 'e screamed. Didn't stop 'til I slit 'is froat," he continued with his story while ladling out three bowls of the stew. It looked and smelled good, but the tale of slaughter was making the boys sick. "Blood gushed out o' 'im like a river, it did. Messy, very messy. But, 'ey, I got a stew out o' 'im, nonetheless."

"Um," Jordan said, "I didn't get through . . . The line died right after I dialed Mack's number."

The man turned and shrugged. "It does 'at from time ta time. Jus' wait a bit an' it'll be workin' again."

Peter, gagging, stood and covered his mouth. "I think we have to go. We really need to get through to someone so we can get home. Our parents will be worried about us."

"Nonsense," the old man said, turning and setting the bowls of stew on the table. "Ya eat firs' and 'en ya can try 'e phone again." The man turned back to the stove and picked up a knife with a long, sharp blade. "Ya want bread wit' yer stew?" He waved the blade as he half-spun back when he didn't get an answer.

"No," Jordan said, squeezing Peter's shoulder harder. "I'm good."

"Me too," Peter muttered.

The man turned back to the stove and unwrapped a loaf of homemade bread and cut himself a slice. He turned back to the table and sat his bowl and the slice of bread down, but still held the knife.

"Sit, son," he said, pointing the sharp object at Jordan.

Jordan quickly pulled out a chair and sat down with wide eyes.

The stove sputtered, drawing the man's attention.

"Fire's gon' out," he said. "I forgot ta bring in wood."

The boys stood at the same time and said in unison, "I'll get it!"

"'Ell that's mighty kind o' ya boys."

"It's no problem at all," Jordan said, shoving Peter toward the door. "We don't mind. It's the least we can do to pay you back for letting us use the phone and feeding us."

They saw the man smile, nod, and sit down at the table as they darted out the door.

"Let's get the hell out of here," Peter said in a harsh whisper as soon as the door was closed behind them.

"I'll second that," Jordan mumbled as they rushed down the dirt path toward the road. "That old dude is crazy!"

Peter nodded in agreement.

When they reached the blacktop they both took off in a light jog; Jordan was still limping, but he was desperate to get away from the shack and closer to someone who might be able to help them.

They'd gone less than half a mile before they came to another dirt driveway, also heading off the road to the right. This one was different from the last in significant ways; it was lined with neatly trimmed bushes, and the grass in the middle and around the bushes was mown.

The boys looked at each other and smiled, slowing down to a walk. Taking deep breaths to calm their hearts, they followed the driveway to a small, well-kept house that immediate made them think of a cottage. The porch light was on and more lights blazed within; they could see people moving around inside.

"This place looks way better than the last one," Peter said with a smile.

"I agree," Jordan said. "That old dude was a fucking freak!"

Still smiling with relief, they mounted the steps to the porch and pressed the little, round, glowing doorbell button; they heard the chimes sound off inside, followed by footsteps coming closer. The door was opened by a middle-aged, bare-footed man in a T-shirt and jean.

"Hi," he said. "Can I help you with something?"

Jordan nodded. "We wrecked a ways back up the road, and we need to use the phone to call a tow truck and a friend to pick us up."

"Oh, yes," the man said, stepping back and welcoming them in, "by all means come in and use the phone." He looked at Peter and frowned. "You okay? Looks like a nasty cut there, on your head."

Peter nodded. "I'm fine."

"Right this way," the man said, closing the door and leading the way further into the house. "You can use the phone in the kitchen. Keri, my wife, doesn't allow shoes on the carpet." He grinned and rolled his eyes as if to say "women."

The boys laughed and followed close behind. Jordan was just picking up the phone to call Mack when a pretty, tall, blonde woman came down the stairs into the hallway, carrying a bundle in a pink blanket. Instantly the boys frowned, wrinkled their noses, and looked around, trying to find the source of a sudden, pungent odor. Peter opened his mouth to say something, but was stopped by a quick elbow to the ribs from Jordan. He scowled, but Jordan gave him a stern look in return, warning him not to mess things up. With a sigh, Peter let it go, after all, the couple didn't seem to smell whatever it was.

"This is my wife, Keri," the man said, stepping over to her and wrapping his arm around her waist, "and this is our daughter Sophie." He bent down and kissed the bundle in the woman's arms and stood up, smiling and proud. "Honey, these boys wrecked their car and needed to use the phone."

"Oh, you poor things!" she exclaimed, and rocked the baby in her arms, making a *shh*ing noise. "Sorry, she cries a lot. I'll take her in the other room so you can make your call in peace."

The boys looked at each other and blinked. They hadn't heard a single peep out of the baby.

"Sorry, guys," the man said. "I better go help her with the baby. Sophie usually gets fussy around bedtime." He headed down the hall to where his wife had disappeared into the living room.

"Ooookay," Peter said, rubbing his forehead, thinking maybe his head injury was more serious than he'd thought.

Jordan had missed the last comment the man made, because he was talking rapidly into the phone, telling Mack they needed a ride.

"Peter," Jordan said, nudging him, "go ask them the address."

He looked at Jordan and shook his head. He searched the kitchen with his eyes until they landed on a stack of mail. He stepped over to the counter and snatched up an envelope and handed it to Jordan, who smiled at his quick thinking. After telling Mack the address, he hung up.

"He's on his way," Jordan said. "Let's go tell these people thanks and head out to the road so he can find us; he said he would be about fifteen minutes."

"Great," Peter said, and followed Jordan down the hall; he ran into Jordan's back when he stopped suddenly. "What the hell, man?" He noticed his friend's eyes were trained on the living room, and his jaw was hanging slack. Stepping to the side, he looked into the room to see what was so fascinating. He instantly gagged and regretted looking.

The woman, Keri, was sitting in a rocker, holding the rotting corpse of a baby to her breast like she was feeding it. The man was sitting on the couch watching with an affectionate express on his face; he looked up and noticed them.

"Did you make your call?" he asked politely.

Keri hurriedly covered her exposed breast and the baby corpse, blushing.

"What the fuck?!" Jordan screamed. "Your wife is playing with a dead baby and you can just sit there and ask how our call went?"

Keri cried out at the outburst and started bawling. The man rose from the couch and headed their way.

Peter tried to quiet Jordan and drag him toward the door, but he wasn't fast enough. The man made it across the room and slammed his fist into Jordan's jaw, knocking him out cold before they could get away. The dead weight of Jordan's body put a sudden halt to the "flee" plan.

Standing there for a moment in shock, Peter looked from his friend to the closed front door. He didn't make his decision fast enough either. Before he knew it, a fist was flying toward his face and then the world when dark with a flash of pain.

~ * ~

"Rick," the woman pleaded. "Let's just kill them and be done with it. When whoever comes to pick them up arrives, we'll just tell them we never saw them. There's no need to draw it out."

"They had no right to talk like that in our house, and about our daughter!" Rick screamed in her face. "Get back upstairs!"

She whimpered.

Peter opened his eyes slowly, hearing and then seeing the couple across a small, dimly lit basement. He noticed Jordan was lying next to him, still unconscious; they were both tied up with coarse rope. He tried not to move, hoping to get something of an idea of what was going on.

Rick walked over to where Jordan lay and pointed down at him with a wooden baseball bat. "I'm gonna wait 'til this little prick wakes up and then I'm going to break every bone in his body before he dies, and then I'm going to do the same to his friend."

Peter closed his eyes as the man, Rick, motioned to him with the bat.

"I'm gonna make both of these little bastards beg and apologize before I end their pitiful little lives."

Keri retreated up the stairs, sobbing pathetically.

Peter heard a door shut and knew they were now alone with the psycho Rick and he couldn't think of a way out.

Rick sat on the bottom step of the wooden staircase and watched them for a while.

Peter made sure he didn't move, and cringed when Jordan woke up with a loud moan.

Psycho Rick jumped to his feet and headed over to him, dragging him up by his hair. "Awake, fucker?" he asked with a vicious leer. "How dare you come into my house and talk to us like that. I don't think your parents beat enough of your insolence out of you when you were younger. I'm gonna make up for it now."

Jordan looked at Rick and blinked rapidly, trying to clear his vision, dangling by his hair from the man's hand.

Rick raised the bat and brought it swiftly down on the backs of Jordan's ankles.

Jordan cried out and his eyes flew wide open as his body jerked from pain and shock.

Rick repeated the blow until he heard the audible crack of bone over the boy's screams.

Peter shook with fear as tears sprang to his eyes. He knew no one was coming to rescue them and that he would be next.

Rick beat Jordan for over an hour before he lost interest in his unconscious body. By that time, Peter was a blubbering idiot.

"Shut up, you," Rick said, kicking him in the stomach. "After I have a rest, you'll get the same."

Peter watched as he wearily trudged up the basement stairs. "Jordan?" he whimpered, and sniffled loudly. "Jordan, answer me, damn it!"

There was no response.

He tried to hold his breath, to see if he could hear Jordan's breathing, but he heard nothing.

Time dragged on forever as Peter waited, shaking with fear, for Rick to return and beat him to death, wishing he would just hurry up and get it over with.

Finally, he heard the basement door open once again, and footfalls on the stairs. They didn't sound heavy enough to be Rick's, and Peter looked up in confusion to see the old man from the shack standing before him with the knife he'd used to cut himself a slice of bread; its blade was dripping with fresh, red blood.

"Oh, no," Peter sighed, and closed his eyes, letting his head fall to the cold cement floor.

The old man knelt down beside him and raised the knife.

Peter flinched and waited for the pain the blade would make as it sank into his flesh.

"Ya all 'ight, son?" he asked as he sliced through the ropes.

"Yeah," Peter said, and nodded, breaking out into fresh sobs of relief.

The man stood and shuffled over to Jordan. ""E's dead," he said in a sorrowful tone, followed by a deep sigh. "Let's get ya outta 'ere. I done called 'e police 'fore I headed ove' 'ere."

They made their way upstairs and Peter saw the lifeless bodies of the middle-aged couple lying in the house. He didn't take the time to look at them closely, just wanting to be out of the house and away from the nightmare.

~ * ~

True to the old man's word, the police showed up almost right away and took their statements, examined the evidence in the house, and called Peter's parents to come and get him.

He learned the next day that there had been many disappearances in that area and the old man had been keeping an eye on the couple the police suspected, and reporting anything odd. With everything the nosey neighbor had provided, they'd still had no solid evidence to act on.

Peter had been the lucky one and had made it out alive, they'd said. But he knew he wasn't as lucky as they said; he had the memory of every single one of his friend's screams before he died. Even though he went through counseling and moved on with his life, at night, in the dark, in the fog, all the memories came back. They never left him, and he was always afraid of back roads and unfamiliar areas, dreading there was someone else out there who wanted to hurt him like they'd hurt Jordan.

Rebecca Besser is the author of the zombie novella, "Undead Drive-Thru, Nurse Blood," and, "Hall of Twelve." She's also a graduate of the Institute of Children's Literature. Her work has appeared in the Coshocton Tribune, Irish Story Playhouse, Spaceports & Spidersilk, joyful!, Soft Whispers, Illuminata, Common Threads, Golden Visions Magazine, Stories That Lift, Super Teacher Worksheets, Living Dead Press Presents Magazine (Iss. 1 & 2), FrightFest eMagazine, An Xmas Charity Ebook, The Stray Branch, and The Undead That Saved Christmas (Vol. 1 & 2) and the Signals From The Void charity anthologies. She has multiple stories in anthologies by Living Dead Press, Wicked East Press, Pill Hill Press, Hidden Thoughts Press, Knight Watch Press, Coscom Entertainment, Crowded Quarantine Publications, and Collaboration of the Dead (projects), and one (each) in an anthology by Post Mortem Press, NorGus Press, Evil Jester Press, and Horrified Press. She also has a poem in an anthology by Naked Snake Press.

She's also an editor and has edited: Dark Dreams: Tales of Terror, Dead Worlds 7: Undead Stories, and

Book of Cannibals 2: The Hunger from Living Dead Press; Earth's End from Wicked East Press; End of Days: An Apocalyptic Anthology (Vol. 4 & 5/co-edited) from Living Dead Press; and she's currently editing It's Weighing On You Mind from Hidden Thoughts Press, and co-editing Beneath The Pretty Lies from Wicked East Press.

When she's not busy writing and/or editing, she's formatting book covers, building/maintaining websites, and writing book reviews.

For more information, visit her website: www.rebeccabesser.com